Orby Shipley

Lyra Eucharistica

Hymns and Verses on the Holy Communion, Ancient and Modern...

Orby Shipley

Lyra Eucharistica
Hymns and Verses on the Holy Communion, Ancient and Modern...

ISBN/EAN: 9783337086312

Printed in Europe, USA, Canada, Australia, Japan

Cover: Foto ©Andreas Hilbeck / pixelio.de

More available books at **www.hansebooks.com**

Lyra Eucharistica.

Lyra Eucharistica:

HYMNS AND VERSES ON
THE HOLY COMMUNION,
ANCIENT AND MODERN;
WITH OTHER POEMS.

EDITED BY

THE REV. ORBY SHIPLEY, M. A.

London:

LONGMAN, GREEN, LONGMAN, ROBERTS,

AND GREEN.

1863.

Preface.

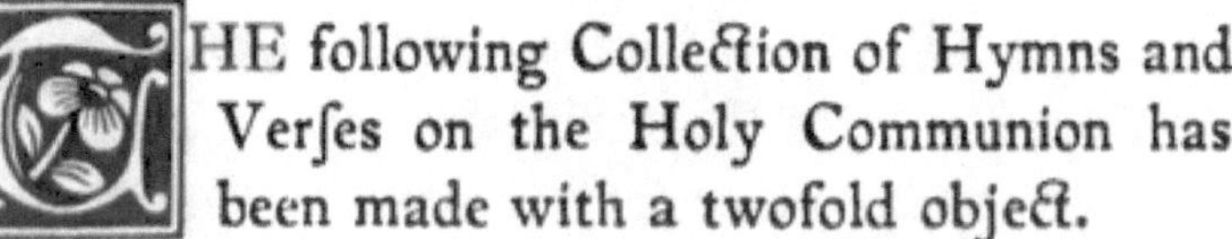

HE following Collection of Hymns and Verses on the Holy Communion has been made with a twofold object.

It is well known, even to thofe who are but little acquainted with the fubject of Hymnology, that there exifts a large number of Hymns, ancient and mediæval, on the Holy Euchariſt. A confiderable number of thefe Hymns have, of late years, been made acceffible to ordinary ftudents in the collections of Daniel, Mone, and others abroad, and by Dr. Neale and other Liturgical fcholars amongft ourfelves. But, in the revived and increafing appreciation of ancient Hymns, thofe which relate to or bear upon the Holy Communion have, for the moft part, been overlooked, or at leaft unheeded. For this difregard of old Euchariſtic Hymns feveral reafons may be given. That it is caufed, not by any lack of devotional fentiment, nor by any abfence of poetic beauty in the Hymns themfelves, will be admitted. But an adequate reaſon may be found in the fact, that the Engliſh Office for Holy Communion is not con-ſidered ſufficiently elaſtic to allow of Hymns, other than thoſe which the Office itſelf already contains, being introduced into Divine Service before the Holy Goſpel for the Day, in the place in which they were formerly ſung.

Hence, although we are indebted, at the pre-ſent day, to ancient Sources for many of the moſt beautiful of our Hymns, which are alſo the moſt popular; yet theſe Hymns, for the moſt part, were compoſed either for the greater Feſtivals of the Church, or for the Commemoration of ſome Holy Day or Seaſon: they were not intended for uſe at Holy Communion. And ſince Hymns ſpe-cially adapted for the Altar Office are ſeldom re-quired, and ſtill leſs often employed, it is only natural that ſuch Hymns from the Latin and the Greek, as well as thoſe of German and other origin, have been but rarely tranſlated into Eng-liſh verſe. The preſent is not the time to expreſs regret for this neglect of Euchariſtic Hymns, nor to venture on an opinion, that, whilſt ſo much talent is devoted, and juſtly, to other muſical portions of Divine Service, it might be well to conſider the re-introduction of Hymns, to be sung congregationally, into the Office for Holy Communion. But, to ſhow how little this claſs of Hymns has been hitherto employed, it may be mentioned that, in the Collection

which has deservedly secured by far the widest
circulation of any Hymnal of the present day,
under the title of *Hymns, Ancient and Modern,*
out of 273 Hymns from all sources, there are
only five printed in the body of the work on the
subject of the Blessed Sacrament, of which two
only are translated from ancient Hymns; although
there are two more, and part of a third, amongst
the Introits, all of which are from ancient Sources.
In the still more recently published Volume
of Hymns, edited by Dr. Kennedy, with the title
of *Hymnologia Christiana,* which contains the
largest number of Hymns, for the use of the
Church, hitherto collected into a single Volume,
viz. 1500 Psalms and Hymns, only one Psalm
and twenty-three Hymns are intended for the
Holy Communion, hardly more than a tithe of
which may be referred to ancient Sources for their
origin.

As my studies have been directed to the English Office for Holy Communion, its history, ri-
tual, and devotions, the question of Eucharistic
Hymns naturally forced itself on my attention;
and I soon found how little we had yet gathered,
in an English form, from that particular portion
of the wide field of ancient Hymnology. It is
true that several Hymns on the Blessed Sacrament have been translated into English verse,
and some of them very frequently.* But they are

* Of the *Pange lingua* there have been at least, and may

chiefly verſions, with more or leſs fidelity and force, by different perſons, of the ſame majeſtic Hymns which, in their original Latin, have attained world-wide renown. The grandeſt and moſt beautiful of theſe Hymns are, in one form or another, familiar to Engliſh readers, but they are few; whilſt many other Hymns and Sequences, which competent judges declare to be only ſecond, and ſometimes not at all inferior, to the inſpirations of S. Thomas Aquinas, have been allowed to remain in the language in which, and, for the moſt part, in the poſition for which, they were originally compoſed.

Until lately, the great body of theſe Sacramental Hymns, even in their original form, has been unknown to all but to Liturgical ſtudents. Of late years, however, a large number have been diſcovered and collected, and have been rendered acceſſible in the Collections mentioned above. But there is good reaſon to believe that we are ſtill unacquainted with the extent of the Church's heritage in Hymnological wealth, as further reſearch is continually bringing to light Hymns previouſly unknown, or long ago forgotten. Many of theſe treaſures, which have been obtained from many parts of Chriſtendom, under the common title of *Sequentiæ Ineditæ*, have

have been many more than ſeventeen or eighteen different verſions or tranſlations, publiſhed of late years; of the *Adoro Te* about thirteen or fourteen.

appeared from time to time, and, it is hoped, will continue to appear, in the pages of the contemporary Periodical, *The Ecclefiologift*.   But in thefe Collections, the Euchariftic Hymns remained in the language in which they were written ; and only the favoured few, chiefly thofe of S. Thomas Aquinas, have found their way, in the vernacular, into Hymn-books or books of Poetry.

Perhaps one of the earlieft attempts during the prefent revival of the tafte for ancient Hymns, (although there have been feveral incidental efforts in previous Centuries,) to popularize Hymns on the Holy Eucharift was made in the year 1839, by the Author of *The Cathedral,* who, in the Volume of *Hymns tranflated from the Parifian Breviary,* tranflated four out of the five well-known Hymns compofed by S. Thomas Aquinas. The fame four Hymns, together with the *Lauda Sion,* were tranflated afrefh, ten years later, by the Rev. E. Cafwall, who to thefe added, in 1858, feveral other Englifh renderings of Sacramental Hymns, which, with his wonted kindnefs, he has allowed to be reprinted, together with feveral other of his Hymns, in *Lyra Euchariftica.* Between thefe two dates feveral other verfions and imitations of one or more of thefe Hymns were iffued. In 1852, Dr. Neale, in *Mediæval Hymns and Sequences,* publifhed two frefh tranflations of the *Adoro Te devote,* and the *Pange lingua,* and to thefe he added a Sacramental Hymn of the vij.

Century; and in a later Volume, *Hymns from the Eastern Church*, he has tranſlated two more, of the vij. and viij. Centuries reſpeƈtively—the three latter of which Hymns, by the great kindneſs of the Tranſlator, appear in the preſent Colleƈtion.

In 1857 *Lauda Syon* was publiſhed, and this, with another publication by the ſame Author, was the firſt effort to eſcape from the accuſtomed groove, in which tranſlators of Hymns on the Holy Communion had hitherto chiefly moved. And in addition to the five uſual Sacramental Hymns, ſix other Hymns, ſome of conſiderable length, have been tranſlated by J. D. Chambers, Eſq., only one of which, it is believed, had previouſly appeared in Engliſh. At the time of its publication, *Lauda Syon* contained the largeſt number of Euchariſtic Hymns that had been colleƈted in one Volume. And it was only by the kindneſs of the Tranſlator, who was ſo good as to allow his Hymns to be reprinted, that a Manual of Devotions for the Altar Office, *The Divine Liturgy*, publiſhed at the cloſe of 1862, contained a ſtill larger colleƈtion of this claſs of Hymns. But the lateſt effort to populariſe Hymns on the Holy Communion, has been made by the "Committee of Clergy," which has lately iſſued ſome valuable Traƈts and Books of Devotion. *Euchariſtic Hymns* is the title of a little Book of ſixteen pages, which contains valuable tranſlations of ſeven Hymns—the greater number of which appeared for the firſt time in an Engliſh verſion. All theſe Hymns have been generouſly placed at my diſpoſal, by the learned Tranſlator, for incorporation into *Lyra Euchariſtica*; and thoſe, of which I have not elſewhere obtained tranſlations, have been thankfully reprinted.

The firſt main object, then, in the publication of *Lyra Euchariſtica*, was the collection into one Book of many of the more beautiful of the ancient and mediæval Hymns on the Bleſſed Sacrament, not only as reprints from Works already publiſhed, but alſo and chiefly of new tranſlations. And this object has been accompliſhed entirely through the kindneſs and inſtrumentality of friends.

The reſult has been this—that out of the large number of Hymns from ancient or mediæval Sources which this Book contains, either directly on the ſubject of the Holy Communion, or indirectly bearing upon it, twenty-ſix or twenty-ſeven are new tranſlations. Some few, indeed, were printed in *The Divine Liturgy* a few months ago; but theſe were kindly undertaken at my ſuggeſtion, and have been rendered into Engliſh in order to form a part of the preſent Collection; ſo that, ſubſtantially, they now appear for the firſt time in the vernacular. And if to theſe be added the Hymns that have been lately publiſhed, it will appear that, during the paſt year, there have been added to our ſtock of Euchariſtic Hymns, from the Greek and Latin, upwards of thirty newly tranſlated Hymns, hitherto unattempted in Engliſh. But although this, in compariſon with previous efforts to introduce ancient Sacramental Hymns into our language, is a large advance on the paſt, yet it is believed that the ſtore, whence theſe Hymns were drawn, is well nigh inexhauſtible, and will amply repay further examination.

The dates of the newly tranſlated or recently publiſhed Hymns from ancient and mediæval Sources contained in this Book extend from the vij. to the xvij. Century; the Hymn written at the lateſt date being compoſed by Santolius of S. Victor, and the two which bear the earlier date being reſpectively, of Latin origin, from the Antiphonary of Banchor, and from a Greek ſource, by S. Andrew, Archbiſhop of Crete. The period, however, which appears to be the richeſt in Euchariſtic Hymns, is that which began in and ſucceeded the age of S. Thomas Aquinas, from the xiij. to the xvj. Centuries; and for the cauſes of this increaſe in the number of Hymns on the Holy Communion at this particular time, there is obvious evidence in the Hiſtory of the Church. The inſtitution of the Feaſt of Corpus Christi, with its Octave of Commemorative Services, of itſelf was ſufficient to create a demand for additional Sacramental Hymns; and many were thoſe who muſt have been inſpired by, even if they did not actually imitate, the compoſitions of the Poet as well as **Doctor** of the Church, who fupplied the authorifed **Hymns** and **Sequences** for that and other Feftivals of Weftern Chriftendom.

" The dates of all thefe **Hymns** cannot be afcertained. In moft cafes, however, it is believed that the date affigned reprefents the Century later than which the **Hymn** was probably **not** written. But if there is uncertainty with reference to the dates, there exifts abfolute ignorance about the Authors of many of the Hymns from ancient Sources in the following Collection ; fo that the Hymns, for the moft part, have to be diftinguifhed by the Locality in which they were difcovered, the Office Book in which they are enfhrined, or even the Collection in which they may now be found. For although the names of S. Andrew of Crete, of S. John Damafcene, of S. Anfelm, S. Bernard, and S. Thomas, of Angelus and Santolius, and of S. Terefa, are attached to fome of the Hymns, yet many more are lacking in any clue for the difcovery of their authorfhip. Moft of them may be claimed by fome Continental Church or Conventual Eftablifhment. Canterbury, York, and Banchor, however, have contributed their quota to the Collection. But the Office Books of Strafburg, Carlfruhe, Paris, Munich, Mayence, Liege, Augfburg, Freifing in Bavaria, Drontheim in Norway, Prague, and the famous Benedictine Abbey of Reichenau, an Ifland in the Lake of Conftance, have fupplied the chief materials for that older portion of *Lyra Euchariſtica* which is now firſt publiſhed.

The ſecond main object in the publication of *Lyra Euchariſtica* was this—the collection into a ſingle Volume of many ſcattered Hymns and Verſes, either already publiſhed, or not yet in print, on the ſubject of the Holy Communion. Thoſe who will give the matter conſideration may remember, that in many recently publiſhed Books of Poetry, amongſt the miſcellaneous Poems, may be found a ſingle one, or more, on the Bleſſed Sacrament. In the Magazines alſo of the day, which have more or leſs of a religious aim, ſuch ſhort pieces of Verſe may often be found. It is true, that neither of theſe two Sources of Euchariſtic Hymns have been drawn from to the extent to which they might, poſſibly, have been made to contribute. Still, there are many Poems thus collected, which have either attained temporary notice and have then been forgotten, or have been printed in Volumes, the ſcarceneſs of which, at the preſent day, proves that they are now but little known, but which many, it is believed, will be glad to poſſeſs in a more acceſſible, as well as more permanent form. There are however, doubtleſs, many more ſingle or fugitive Hymns or Poems of this deſcription which might have been added, and have been overlooked ; and I ſhall feel it to be a kindneſs, if thoſe, who feel diſpoſed, will take the trouble to draw my attention to any such Verses, published during the last thirty or forty years.

In addition to these reprints, there are many Hymns in the following pages which are neither forgotten nor scarce. And *Lyra Eucharistica* is indebted to several Collections of the present day for some of the most beautiful of its Poems. The only difficulty in the selection was to know where to stop, or what to abstain from taking, where permission was kindly given to choose. But in a Collection which aimed to a certain extent at completeness, it was thought wise to admit many Hymns well known and deservedly appreciated, which otherwise it would have been needless to reprint.

To these two classes of modern Hymns and Verses has been added another, that of original and unpublished Poems. And this is a distinction where a distinction is not needless. For whilst *Lyra Eucharistica* contains several Original Hymns, written expressly (and with much kindness) for this Work, it also contains many which, although hitherto unpublished, were not written expressly for it. It is perhaps not strange, that in the present wide-spread teaching of the true Doctrine of the Holy Communion, and in the consequent revived dignity and honour in which It is esteemed, and the care and frequency with which It is celebrated, the minds of many, who are capable of it, should find relief from devotion and meditation on the Myſtery of the Holy Euchariſt, in poetic compoſition. Such, however, is the faƈt: and it needed only the knowledge that ſuch a Colleƈtion of Poems as *Lyra Euchariſtica* was contemplated, to produce, from many quarters, Hymns, written it may be long ago, which have been, with much courteſy, placed at my diſpoſal. Here, again, it is poſſible that ſome Readers may feel inclined to communicate with me, with a view, at ſome future time, of publiſhing Additional Hymns to the preſent Volume. I ſhall be very grateful for, and will give every conſideration to, ſuch communications.

This is the ſecond objeƈt with which *Lyra Euchariſtica* was printed ; and, as far as regards unprinted Verſes, the reſult has been this, that ſix or ſeven-and-twenty original or unpubliſhed Hymns have been added to our formerly but ſcanty ſtock of Poems on the Bleſſed Sacrament. And all of theſe, I have to acknowledge with gratitude, are due to the kindneſs and courteſy of known or unknown friends.

In addition to Hymns from the Sources indicated above, there have been added ſeveral Hymns of much beauty from the German, both new tranſlations, and reprints of former tranſlations. Hymns of German Origin are generally full of devotional beauty ; and I only regret that *Lyra Euchariſtica* poſſeſſes ſo few ſpecimens of Communion Hymns from that Source. The paucity of tranſlations, however, of Hymns on the Holy Communion, which has been obſerved in the caſe of ancient and mediæval Hymns, is equally apparent in that of Hymns from the German. For whilſt *Sacred Hymns from the German*, by Miſs Cox, contains but a ſingle Euchariſtic Hymn, Miſs Winkworth's *Lyra Germanica* poſſeſſes only ſeven Hymns out of about 225 (in both ſeries), and the volume publiſhed under the title of *Hymns from the Land of Luther* has only one Poem ſpecially on the ſubjeƈt of Holy Communion : all of which tranſlations have been kindly placed at my diſpoſal, and moſt of which will be found below. There will alſo be found nine or ten new tranſlations, by friends, from the German, which have not previouſly been publiſhed.

Laſtly, ſcattered through the Colleƈtion, there are Hymns and Verſes, original, newly tranſlated, and reprinted, which, although they are not direƈtly Euchariſtic in charaƈter, are indireƈtly conneƈted with the Doƈtrine of Sacrifice which is involved in the Holy Communion, or may be made to bear an Euchariſtic ſignification. For theſe too, I owe many thanks to ſeveral Contributors ; and it is hoped that theſe miſcellaneous Hymns, whilſt not out of harmony with the ſubjeƈt-matter of the Volume, will tend to prevent too much ſameneſs in its treatment.

Thus I have endeavoured to combine Hymns ancient and modern, and by the mutual contraſt to enhance the relative value of both. I venture to have my own private opinion on the refpective merits and beauty of the two claffes of Hymns, to which it would be uncourteous in the prefence of ancient tranflated Hymns and modern original ones—and both at the hands of friends—to give expreffion. But the union of the two will be beneficial to both. The fubjective devotion and tendernefs of modern Hymns, will be ftrengthened by the definite Theological ftatements of thofe of ancient and mediæval origin ; and the fyftematic Theology and the enunciation of the higheft objective Truths in the old Hymns, will be foftened and brought home to the inner confcioufnefs by the contemplative elements in the new. In addition to this double benefit, monotony and famenefs will be avoided, which could hardly fail to refult from a Collection of Hymns on the Holy Communion from any one fingle Source : whilft, in the cafe of *Lyra Euchariftica*, additional variety is enfured by the introduction of mifcellaneous Hymns, not out of harmony with thofe with which they come in contact.

I have now to exprefs my fincere gratitude to all the many friends who have affifted me in the compilation of *Lyra Euchariftica*. Where all have been kind, it would be invidious to refer to any, unlefs reference is made, in detail, to all. The names of all thofe to whom I am indebted will be found below, in the *Index of the Sources*

of the Hymns—of all thofe, at leaft, whofe names
I am at liberty to mention. The remainder are
indicated by initial letters. And I beg that all
will be fo good as to accept individually, the
thankful acknowledgments which are thus made
collectively : for my beft thanks are due to thofe
who have helped me either as Authors, with their
talents, in the original portions of the Book, or
with their kind permiffion, in the cafe of thofe
Hymns which have been reprinted : or as Publifhers, with their generous leave to make ufe of
their literary property.

In all cafes, where it was either practicable or
needful, and in many in which it was not necef-
fary, I have obtained permiffion from thofe con-
cerned to reprint the Hymns which are now re-
publifhed. Such a courfe, I conceive to be only
courteous ; whilft the breach of it involves the
breach of a principle—intrinfically—of honefty,
which in thefe days fometimes leads to difagreeable
contingencies. At the fame time, I cannot but
exprefs an opinion—whilft fully allowing the legal
right of either Publifher or Author to refufe permiffion, and alfo admitting my deep obligations
and debt of gratitude to thofe who with liberal
generofity have aided me in this Compilation—
that Devotional Literature, be it profe or poetry,
is the common heritage of a common Chriftianity,
and that they are to be reprehended who would
throw obftacles in the way of a wider circulation

of a form of words, which tends to make men more holy and juſt and good. Of courſe there are limits even to religious poaching for the benefit of Souls; and I am aware that my view is in oppoſition to the mercantile view of the caſe. I may now, however, venture to ſay, without the chance of being miſtaken, with regard to the Hymns now firſt publiſhed in this Collection, that they are copy-right : and I may add, at the requeſt of a Contributor, that permiſſion to reprint any of the original Hymns muſt be made to myſelf. At the worſt, ſuch an announcement will be regarded as the reſult of pardonable vanity on behalf of the contributions of friends.

All the Hymns which have been reprinted in the following pages, have been reprinted *verbatim*, except in a few inſtances of adaptation, which have been duly acknowledged. Into the queſtion of the morality of altering the Hymns of others, I will not enter. In the caſe of living Authors, there appears to be only one alternative to be adopted—either to obtain permiſſion or to abſtain from altering. In the caſe of Hymns to be uſed in Divine Worſhip, in one generation, which were the offſpring of a former, it ſeems deſirable to relax the ſterner principle. Of late, it has been the faſhion to decry all alteration. I apprehend this to be a miſtake. Only a Collector knows the pang which reſults from a deciſion to omit ſome beautiful Hymn from a Collection, on account of ſome trivial miſtake in taſte or fault in rhyme, which a ftroke of the pen would remedy, or reftore to accordance with the wonted vocabulary of the day. Such felf-command I have had to exercife ; at the fame time, I muft allow, (to anticipate criticifm) that I am confcious of fome things I would fee otherwife, in the prefent Collection. But as this Volume was not compiled with a view to defy critical acumen, and as it does not afpire to poetic infallibility, but was prepared with a view to Religious and Devotional edification, I have been the lefs careful to exercife a rigid cenforfhip in this particular. Still, I have not added fome . Hymns, which I would gladly have added ; and I have not confidered the omiffion of verfes or ftanzas to deferve the lafh adminiftered to thofe, who undertake to improve upon the compofitions of their friends. Thofe who ufe the lafh, however, fhould confider the temptation—and fhould apply it accordingly. On this fubject, I have only to add, that as a rule, the Hymns in this Volume are not meant for public worfhip, nor for finging. Some of the Verfes, it is true, are intended for both purpofes ; and fome have either had mufic fet to them, or have themfelves been written for mufic.

Nothing, it is maintained, has been printed in *Lyra Eucharifica* which is not in accordance with the Teaching of the Church of England, on the Myftery which forms the fubject of the Collection. This is no place for controverfy ; but it appears to me, that we are differently placed with reference to thoſe with whom we have the misfortune to differ, and between which, Eccleſiaſtically, we find ourſelves placed. And whilſt I have no heſitation to uſe the words of thoſe with whom I agree ſubſtantially on the Doctrine of the Real Preſence, and rejoice to be allowed to do ſo, be they in what Branch of the Church they may; it ſeems to me, on the other hand, to be unreal to employ a form of words, which, though in ſound they can be ſubſcribed, yet in eſſence are not intended to convey the meaning which they may be made to bear. Hence, I have reluctantly omitted many beautiful Hymns. But if the opportunity is afforded, I ſhould rejoice to be able to include the Verſes to which I refer, amongſt the Additional Hymns which are alluded to above. The Hymns tranſlated from the German ſtand, Theologically, upon a different footing. But even if it be inſiſted that their inſertion is inconſiſtent, I ſhall claim an exception on behalf of the few that are printed, which are not of German Catholic origin; whilſt, to prevent miſtake, I may ſtate that, to my mind, the ſcruples in the uſe of Hymns by thoſe of different Creeds, which I have expreſſed, only refer to compoſitions on ſubjects wherein oppoſing Doctrines are brought into colliſion, ſuch as the ſubject of the Holy Communion. On other ſubjects, I ſhould be ſorry to deny myſelf the benefit to be derived from a good Hymn, ſimply becauſe it was written by one with whom I was unable, dogmatically, to agree.

In the event of *Lyra Euchariftica* proving a fuccefs, in a bufinefs point of view, the Publifhers are willing to iffue a fifter Volume, compiled upon the fame principles as the prefent work—with this difference, that I fhould wifh to be allowed to add Hymns and Verfes from the Sources which I have felt myfelf debarred from ufing on the prefent occafion. The reafon to which I have referred would not hold good in the cafe of a felection of Hymns on the Life of our Bleffed Lord; and though I do not apprehend there will be a large proportion of Hymns from other Sources, than thofe from which this work is drawn, yet, it is propofed to admit of a fomewhat wider latitude in the compilation. The title fuggefted for the future Collection is *Lyra Meffianica*; and the fub-ject-matter of the Hymns will be the leading Events and chief Myfteries in the Life of Christ, arranged in accordance with the fequence of the Seafons and Feftivals of the Church. I have already collected much material for the propofed publication; and if thefe lines reach the eye of any who feel difpofed to help me carry it into effect, either with tranflations from the Latin, Greek, German, or other languages, or with original pieces, or again with formerly printed Verfes, I fhall be greatly obliged for fuch affiftance. And I may ftate, roughly and in outline, that the fcope of the propofed Collection will be as follows, and that *Lyra Meffianica*, if I am allowed to publifh it, will contain Hymns, amongft others, on the Advent of our Bleffed LORD, the Annunciation, the Nativity, the Epiphany, the Holy Childhood, perhaps on the Miniftry, on the Paffion, Crucifixion, and Entombment, the Refurrection, the Forty Days after, and the Afcenfion, and poffibly on the glorified Life in Heaven, and the Second Advent.

The Hymns in *Lyra Euchariftica* have been arranged according to the fivefold Divifion into which the Englifh Office for the Holy Communion is divifible. In many cafes this divifion is arbitrary. But it was thought better to attempt fome arrangement, even an imperfect one, than to print the Hymns under no fyftem; and to arrange them according to their fubject-matter, as far as poffible, rather than in their chronological order, or under the headings of their Authors' or Tranflators' names. The Altar Office has ever been divifible into five Ritualiftic portions; and although the Office in the Book of Common Prayer has received feveral additions to, and has fuffered from many tranfpofitions in its component parts, from its earlier and purer form, yet thefe five Divifions can ftill be diftinctly traced. The Introduction reaches from the beginning of the Office to the Creed. Then follows the Oblation, which includes the Offering of the Elements, and the collection of the Alms, and reaches to

Prayer of Humble Acce/s. Thirdly, comes the
/acred Act of Con/ecration, or the Canon, as it
was anciently termed. After that, the Communion of the People follows : and the Office is
concluded with the Thank/giving. Now the fir/t
and la/t Divi/ions of the Office are ea/ily /upplied
with Hymns; for many of the Euchari/tic Hymns
were compo/ed for u/e either in Preparation for,
or in Thank/giving after the Ble//ed Sacrament.
In the Part entitled the Con/ecration, it was
thought well that the majority of the Hymns
/hould be from ancient or mediæval Sources.
The difficulty of arrangement is therefore chiefly
confined to the /econd and fourth Parts. And in
the/e two Divi/ions, German Hymns and reprinted
ones have been combined with original Ver/es and
tran/lations from the Latin or Greek, in /uch a
manner as to produce the lea/t amount of /ame-
ne/s in the combination.

I am re/pon/ible, not only for the arrangement
of the Hymns, but al/o for the Titles and for
the /election of the Texts at the head of mo/t of
the Poems. Many, both of the Texts and the
Titles of tho/e Hymns that are reprinted, are re-
produced from the Sources whence they are derived ; but many al/o are new /elections. The
tran/lations have been made on no one /y/tem.
The Collection contains /pecimens of many kinds
of rendering: and literal ver/ions have been placed
/ide by /ide with tho/e that are freer in tran/lation,

and which ſeek to convey the ſenſe of the original, rather in correſponding, than in abſolutely equivalent terms. As a rule, duplicate tranſlations of the ſame Hymns have not been inſerted ; but in a few caſes this rule has been relaxed in favour of ſome Verſes in very different ſtyles of rendering.

I muſt apologiſe for this egotiſtical and lengthy Preface. As it is the only portion of *Lyra Euchariſtica* I contribute—although the pleaſure of collecting and arranging the whole Volume has been mine—perhaps ſome excuſe may be made for both faults. At leaſt the Reader has the remedy in his own hands, and may proceed at once to the main portion of the Book—a courſe, of which I certainly ſhall not complain.

ORBY SHIPLEY.

S. Barnabas' Day,
   A.D. 1863.

Contents.

PART I.

THE PREPARATION.

PART II.

THE OBLATION.

PART IV.

THE COMMUNION.

PART V.

THE THANKSGIVING.

ERRATA.

Page xxxv, laſt line, *for* " 206 " *read* " 207."

Page 110, line 5, *for* " Behold" *read* " Behold !"

Page 110, line 8, *for* " this earthly Germ" *read* " the earthly Sum."

Page 122, line 15, *for* " humbling" *read* " trembling."

Page 126, lines 8, 12, and 14, *for* " Hail !" " Hail !" *and* " Thou" *read in each* " O."

Page 144, *inſtead* of lines 5 and 6 *read*
> " Ranſom, Guide, Redemption free,
> Now our Satisfaction be."

Page 173, line 14, *for* " befitting" *read* " be fitting."

Page 207, laſt line but 5, *for* " Victory" *read* " Victor."

Page 232, line 19, *for* " Gift" *read* " Gifts."

Index of Sources, No. 60, *add* " Baſed on a tranſlation in *The Prieſt to the Altar*, a privately printed Manual for Holy Communion."

Ditto, No. 118, *for* " Unknown" *read* " Baſed on a Hymn of C. Weſley, 1745, by an unknown writer."

Ditto, No. 164, *add* " The original Sequence is printed in the *Eccleſiologiſt*, vol. xix. 1858."

Lyra Eucharistica.

Hymns and Verses on the Holy Communion.

PART I.

THE PREPARATION.

An Ancient Eucharistic Hymn.

Quo me, Deus, amore.

MY GOD, what lack I more when
    Thou doſt bleſs?
    Deep calleth unto deep when Thou
    Bendeſt from Heav'n o'er my un-
        worthineſs
Haſtening to pay its vow;
For me Thou comeſt to Thy Altar holy,
    For me—O Love beyond all ken—
Prieſt of the Moſt High God, yet Victim lowly,
    Giver, yet Gift to men.

Here no flain beafts, nor birds of air are refting,
 Not with earth's fruits the Soul is fed,
But Sweets of Paradife, Thy Love attefting,
  Here are full lavifhèd;
With love for that vaft Love, with ftrong felf-
   loathing
 Thee in this Sacrament we hail;
Thee we do worfhip, clothed in that poor Clothing,
 Veiled in that lowly Veil.

Farewell then all! The Lamb's bleft Supper
   waiteth;
 Farewell then all I loved before!
Farewell, farewell for aye! my heart repeateth,
 Ye have my heart no more:
O Bethlehem, whence fprings the Bread of
   Heaven,
 O Jordan, whence is Drink Divine,
Not earthly hufks, nor Abana's wave be given,
 Only my LORD be mine.

Sweet is the grape in fair Engaddi's valley,
 Sweet was the Manna fent to blefs
The weary fainting people, wandering daily
  In the great wildernefs;
But Thou, O Flour of Wheat, O Vine of Glad-
   nefs,
 Only for Thee I thirft. Do Thou
Come to Thy lowlieft Graft and cheer his fadnefs,
 So fhall he pay his vow.

The Precious Blood.

Viva! Viva! Gesu, *che per mio bene.*

HAIL, Jesus, hail! Who for my ſake,
　　Sweet Blood from Mary's Veins didſt
　　　　take,
　　　　And ſhed It all for me ;
Oh, bleſſed by my Saviour's Blood,
My Life, my Light, my only Good,
　　　　To all Eternity.

To endleſs ages let us praiſe
The Precious Blood, Whoſe Price could raiſe
　　　　The world from wrath and ſin ;
Whoſe Streams our inward thirſt appeaſe,
And heal the ſinner's worſt diſeaſe,
　　　　If he but bathe therein.

O Sweeteſt Blood, that can implore
Pardon of God, and Heaven reſtore,
　　　　The Heaven which ſin had loſt ;
While Abel's blood for vengeance pleads,
What Jesus ſheds ſtill intercedes
　　　　For thoſe who wrong Him moſt.

Oh, to be ſprinkled from the wells
Of Christ's own Sacred Blood, excels
　　　　Earth's beſt and higheſt bliſs ;

The minifters of Wrath Divine
Hurt not the happy hearts that fhine
    With thofe red Drops of His.

Ah, there is joy amid the Saints,
And Hell's defpairing courage faints
    When this fweet fong we raife ;
Oh, louder then, and louder ftill,
Earth with one mighty chorus fill,
    The Precious BLOOD to praife.

Conformity of the human Will to the Will Divine.

Hier ift mein Herz.
MY SON, GIVE ME THINE HEART.

HERE is my heart—my GOD, I give it
    Thee ;
    I heard Thee call and fay—
Not to the world, My Child, but unto
    Me—
I heard, and will obey :
Here is love's offering to my King,
Which in glad facrifice I bring—
    Here is my heart.

Here is my heart—furely the gift, though poor,
    My GOD will not defpife ;
Vainly and long I fought to make it pure
    To meet Thy fearching Eyes ;

Corrupted firſt in Adam's fall,
The ſtains of ſin pollute it all—
    My guilty heart.

Here is my heart—my heart ſo hard before,
    Now by Thy Grace made meet,
Yet bruiſed and wearied it can only pour
    Its anguiſh at Thy Feet :
It groans beneath the weight of ſin,
It ſighs Salvation's joy to win—
    My mourning heart.

Here is my heart—in CHRIST my longings end,
    Near to His Croſs it draws ;
It ſays—Thou art my portion, O my Friend,
    Thy BLOOD my Ranſom was :
And in the SAVIOUR it has found
What bleſſedneſs and peace abound—
    My truſting heart.

Here is my heart—Ah, HOLY SPIRIT, come
    Its nature to renew,
And conſecrate it wholly to Thy home
    A temple fair and true :
Teach it to love and ſerve Thee more,
To fear Thee, truſt Thee, and adore—
    My cleanſèd heart.

Here is my heart—it trembles to draw near
    The Glory of Thy Throne :
Give it the ſhining Robe Thy ſervants wear
    Of Righteouſneſs Thine Own :

Its pride and folly chaſe away,
And all its vanity, I pray—
  My humbled heart.

Here is my heart—teach it, O LORD, to cling
  In gladneſs unto Thee;
And in the day of ſorrow ſtill to ſing—
  Welcome, my GOD's decree;
Believing all its journey through
That Thou art Wiſe, and Juſt, and True—
  My waiting heart.

Here is my heart—O Friend of friends be near
  To make each tempter fly;
And when my lateſt foe I wait with fear
  Give me the victory:
Gladly on Thy Love repoſing,
Let me ſay when life is cloſing—
  Here is my heart.

Draw near with Faith.

Let us draw near with a true heart, in full
aſſurance of faith.

UNTO Thy holy Altar, LORD,
  Our heads and hearts bowed low,
Where Thou art moſt to be adored,
  We come Thy Grace to know.
Wearied and wounded in our ſtrife
  With Satan and with ſin,

We come to Thee, the Bread of Life,
New ſtrength and hope to win.

We do not aſk how it can be,
That Thou Thyſelf ſhouldſt give
Into our hands and hearts ; but we
Receive Thee there, and live.
Oh, dwell within us when we turn
Back on our earthly way,
And may we, by Thy Preſence, learn
To love Thee more each day.

A Prayer in Preparation for the Holy Communion, of the xv. Century.

Salve! Saluberrima.

HAIL! Thou, Who from Heaven on high
Health to all ſickneſs beareſt ;
Hail! Unto the darkened eye
Thou of all light the faireſt.

Hail! Deſire which life tranſcends
Of all Thy Saints departed ;
Hail! Who to Thy loving friends
Art e'er the Loving-hearted.

Hail! Thou Bread of Angels bleſt,
Moſt ſweet and ever-precious ;
Hail! Who with Divineſt taſte
Doſt in Thy Paths refreſh us.

The Preparation.

Thou in very truth art He,
  Whom my whole Soul defireth;
God and Man I worfhip Thee,
  To Thee my faith afpireth.

When in confcience or in thought
  Guilt or dark error dwelleth,
Faith, by Thy dear Prefence brought,
  All gloom and woe difpelleth.

Make me all the fervour feel
  Of that Thy Fire Divineft;
Now Thyfelf unfeen reveal,
  Who e'er in fecret fhineft.

Let the clouds, which dim my Soul,
  Before Thy genial Splendour,
Hence away far diftant roll,
  And leave it pure and tender.

Come, O Christ, King ever bleft,
  Come, Thou our Confolation,
In my heart a welcome Gueft
  Fix Thy glad habitation.

May that golden fhaft of Love,
  Which once fo deeply fmote Thee,
And from Heaven, Thy Throne above,
  Into this fad world brought Thee,

Wound anew Thy tender Heart,
   That Thou in Glory reigning,
Mayſt to me Thy SELF impart,
   From all Thy Wrath refraining.

Here Thy bleſſed ſojourn make,
   Fragrance and Joy diffuſing ;
Reſt in my ſad boſom take,
   Therein Thy manſion chooſing.

GOD of Love and Clemency,
   Now to Thyſelf unite me ;
And, tranſgreſſor though I be,
   Ne'er in diſpleaſure ſlight me.

LORD, of Thee this Gift I claim,
   For this one Mercy pleading ;
For Thine ever-bleſſed Name,
   For that Thy Love exceeding,

Which erſt made Thee deign to be
   Of our frail fleſh partaker ;
With Grace and Kindneſs viſit me
   Thy ſervant, O my Maker.

Chooſe me for thy dwelling-place
   O GOD of my Salvation ;
Fold my heart in Thine Embrace,
   Sweet Gueſt, take here Thy ſtation.

Think not how I am, with Thee,
    A vile and weak tranfgreffor;
Rather how, made MAN, for me,
    Thou art an Interceffor.

By that mighty Love which moved
    Thee on that Crofs afcending,
When thereon Thy Limbs beloved
    Thou waft meekly bending;

So with loving kind Embrace
    Caft now Thine Arms around me;
And by the bounties of Thy Grace
    Give proof that I have found Thee.

Hither come with joyful fpeed,
    Oh, hafte Thee here to meet me;
Give Thyfelf to me indeed
    A finner, I entreat Thee.

A Prayer to the Lord Jefus in the Bleffed Sacrament.

My Soul hath a defire and longing to enter into the Courts of the LORD.

LORD, to Thine Altar let me go,
    The child of wearinefs and woe,
      My Home to find;
From fin, and fenfe, and felf fet free,

Abſorbed alone in love to Thee,
Able to leave in liberty
    This world behind.

Jesus, be Thou my Heavenly Food,
Sweet Source Divine of every Good,
    Centre of Reſt;
One with Thy Heart let me be found,
Proſtrate upon that holy Ground,
Where Grace, and Peace, and Life abound,
    Drawn from Thy Breaſt.

There let me lean, and live, and lie,
As faſt the fleeting moments fly,
    Sands in a glaſs,
Which Time may ſhake with reſtleſs hand,
Yet only at Thine Own Command,
Till to a dearer, happier Land,
    My Soul ſhall paſs.

Then, then unveiled wilt Thou appear
To thoſe, who walking with Thee here,
    Theſe wilds have trod,
In faith, that with the Cherubim,
The Saints, and Hoſts of Seraphim,
They too may join th' eternal Hymn
    To Thee, O God.

The Morning of Reception.

Let a man examine himself, and so let him eat of that
Bread and drink of that Cup.

I T' is a day of fear :
　　Riſe up betimes, go forth alone
　　With tongue faſt ſealed and heart bowed
　　　　down,
　Becauſe Thy LORD is near.

　　Leave not thy thoughts to roam
　Hither and thither, where they would ;
　Leſt fretful cares on thee ſhould crowd,
　　Forgetful of thy Home.

　　Let not thine eye go free ;
　Look on the earth beneath thy feet,
　The pit that for thy ſins was meet,
　　Had GOD been juſt with thee.

　　Bethink thee of thy ſin ;
　A ſtifling cloud, a feſtering ſore,
　A rotting canker at the core,
　　That gnaws thy heart within.

　　Good art thou to the ſight ;
　But would thy cheek be dry as now,
　As gay thy ſmile, as bright thy brow,
　　If all were brought to light ?

Yet, not in gloomy ſadneſs
Be thy heart bowed and eye down caſt;
Is not the night of ſorrow paſt?
   Is't not a morn of gladneſs?

Think on the Holy Feaſt,
On His dear Love and gracious Name
Who ſanctifies Himſelf, the ſame
   Both Sacrifice and Prieſt.

Go, and be One with Him;
Dwell thou in Him, and He in thee,
Him freely love Who ſets thee free,
   Though but in ſhadow dim.

For, it ſhall not be ſo
In that great Day, when faithful Souls,
Whom fleſh doth ſway and ſin controls,
   As they are known ſhall know:

To be for ever One
With Him, Whom with the FATHER High,
And SPIRIT, Angels tremblingly
   Adore as GOD alone.

Bleſs, LORD, Thy Child, oh, bleſs;
Strengthen my weakneſs; ſoothe my grief;
Forgive and help mine unbelief;
   Reſtore my faithleſſneſs.

To God, Whom all adore,
The Father, Son, and Comforter,
Who is before all creatures were,
Be Glory evermore.

An Ancient Communion Hymn.

Salve, festa Dies!

HAIL, festal Day! for evermore adored,
The Virgin Church salutes her Bride-
groom Lord.
Hail, festal Day!

This is God's Palace, House of Peace and Health,
Here the poor enter to their Father's Wealth.
Hail, festal Day!

David's Son is here—Who hath made us kin
To God and man, these Mother walls within.
Hail, festal Day!

Ye are the wedded Band, the nuptial Ring,
If keeping truth, your Heavenly Troth ye bring.
Hail, festal Day!

Here new Jerusalem descendeth bright,
Fresh deck'd with jewels from the Halls of Light.
Hail, festal Day!

Here fruits of Faith, that ſpring from holy Love,
The King of Juſtice waters from above.
                    Hail, feſtal Day!

This, David's Tower of Strength—Oh, run with
        ſpeed,
Here ſhalt thou find the Pledge of Heaven indeed.
                    Hail, feſtal Day!

This is GOD's Ark, that, while the faithful roam,
Bears them o'er trembling waters ſafely Home.
                    Hail, feſtal Day!

𝕿𝖍𝖊 𝕾𝖆𝖈𝖗𝖊𝖉 𝕳𝖚𝖒𝖆𝖓𝖎𝖙𝖞 𝖔𝖋 𝕵𝖊𝖘𝖚𝖘 𝖙𝖍𝖊 𝕻𝖗𝖎𝖓𝖈𝖎𝖕𝖑𝖊 𝖔𝖋 𝕰𝖙𝖊𝖗𝖓𝖆𝖑 𝕷𝖎𝖋𝖊.

Mein JESU, *der du vor dem Scheiden.*

LORD, Who on that laſt ſad eve,
    Ere Thou didſt die to ſave our race,
    Fruits of Thy painful Death didſt leave,
    In this New-cov'nant Meal of Grace;
For this, of all Thy Gifts the beſt,
Thy Holy Name be praiſed and bleſt.

New Life, from Thy Life-giving BLOOD,
    This Sacramental Cup beſtows;
We take and eat this hallow'd Food
    In memory of Thy dying Woes;
Thy Wounds, Thy Croſs, Thy bitter Pain,
Our thoughts recall them all again.

We hail an added Sign and Seal
    Anew on burdened hearts impreſſed,
That Thy deep Wounds our wound can heal:
    Thy Love has ſet our fears at reſt,
Cancelled the debt we could not pay,
Torn up and thrown the bond away.

The cords more cloſely here we tie,
    That faithful Souls with Thee unite ;
The flame of Love mounts up on high,
    And rules with all-ſubduing might :
The Grace ſuch ſacred hours afford,
Makes us more one with Thee, O LORD.

Through that new Strength Thy BODY gives,
    That quick'ning Power Thy BLOOD imparts,
The failing inner Life revives,
    In gueſts who have believing hearts :
With freſh reſolve, once more begin
The work of Faith, the ſtrife with ſin.

With all Thy Members, CHRIST, our Head,
    We cheriſh thus Communion ſweet ;
To drink One Cup, to eat One Bread,
    Renders our Union more complete :
One Heart, one Soul, unite our band
Poſſeſſors of this Cov'nant land.

Thy FLESH a ſolemn Pledge conveys,
    That our weak fleſh, though here it dies,

Like herbs brought forth by dews and rays,
  A glorious body ſhall ariſe ;
And when this pilgrim ſtate is o'er,
Shall live with Thee for evermore.

O LAMB of GOD, ſuch precious Gifts
  Are in this holy Banquet ſtored,
The Soul from earth to Heav'n it lifts
  In faith to feed at this Thy Board :
How high the Feaſt, the gain how vaſt,
Where Thou Thyſelf art our Repaſt.

𝔄 𝔖equence of the xvi. Century.

Hodiernæ Lux diei.

THE ſun that lights this happy day
  For riſen man on toil intent,
For us lights up a ſurer ray,
  Renews the Holy Sacrament,
Where ever contrite Love hath place,
A healing Balm, a quickening Grace.

To-day th' eternal Promiſe comes,
  Th' eternal Hand is open ſpread,
We ſcarcely looked for falling Crumbs,
  We win the children's Pilgrim-Bread ;
    As Bread of old from Heav'n was ſent,
    He comes, a Gift moſt excellent.

C

That was the bread which Moſes gave
  The tribes in Sinai's wilderneſs,
Fruit of a Law which could not ſave—
  This is the Bread of Angels; This
    He gave, Who ſits upon Heav'n's Throne,
    At His Laſt Supper to His Own.

Haſt thou a Spirit pure and free
  In yearnings, hating nought but ſin?
Life of the world yet giv'n for thee,
  This Bread renews the heart within;
    Vain ſuch a Myſtery to ſhow
    Are eyes. Have Faith—and thou ſhalt know.

Hail! Bread Immortal, Hail! Sweet Food,
  Sweet unto thoſe Thou feedeſt thus;
Hail! Everlaſting LAMB, Whoſe BLOOD
  Is our Salvation. Come to us;
    We thirſt; we tremble; we implore
    Thy Grace. Oh, feed us evermore.

A Proceſſional Hymn.

The LORD *ſhall ſuddenly come to His Temple.*

IN the Name of GOD the FATHER,
  In the Name of GOD the SON,
  In the Name of GOD the SPIRIT,
    ONE in THREE, and THREE in ONE,

In the Name Which higheſt Angels
   Speak not ere they veil their face,
Crying—Holy, Holy, Holy,
   Come we to this ſacred Place.

Lo, in wondrous Condeſcenſion,
   Jesus ſeeks His Altar-throne ;
Though in lively Symbols hidden,
   Faith and Love His Preſence own :
When the Lord His Temple viſits,
   Let the liſt'ning earth be ſtill ;
May the Spirit's ſweet Indwelling
   Each believing heart fulfil.

Here, in Figure repreſented,
   See the Paſſion once again ;
Here, behold, the Lamb moſt Holy,
   As for our Redemption ſlain ;
Here the Saviour's Body broken,
   Here the Blood Which Jesus ſhed—
Myſtic Food of Life Eternal—
   See, for our Refreſhment ſpread.

Here ſhall higheſt praiſe be offered,
   Here ſhall meekeſt prayer be poured,
Here with Body, Soul, and Spirit,
   God Incarnate be adored :
Holy Jesu, for Thy Coming,
   May Thy Love our hearts prepare ;
Thine we fain would have them wholly,
   Enter, Lord, and tarry there.

The Holy Feast.

Come, for all things are now ready.

LO, the Feaſt is ſpread to-day,
Jesus ſummons, come away
From the vanity of life,
From the ſounds of mirth or ſtrife,
To the Feaſt by Jesus given,
Come and taſte the Bread of Heaven.

Why, with proud excuſe and vain,
Spurn His Mercy once again?
From amidſt life's ſocial ties,
From the farm and merchandiſe,
Come, for all is now prepared;
Freely given, be freely ſhared.

Bleſſed are the lips that taſte
Our Redeemer's Marriage-feaſt;
Bleſſed, who on Him ſhall feed,
Bread of Life, and Drink indeed;
Bleſſed, for their thirſt is o'er;
They ſhall never hunger more.

Make them once again your choice;
Hear to-day His calling Voice:
Servants, do your Maſter's Will;
Bidden Gueſts, His Table fill;
Come, before His Wrath ſhall ſwear—
Ye ſhall never enter there.

An Exhortation to the Soul to receive the Body of her Lord, of the xv. Century.

Eia, dulcis Anima.

HASTE my Soul, thou ſiſter ſweet,
    Who all my being ſhareſt,
    For thy Spouſe a chamber meet
      Now ſee that thou prepareſt ;
For a kind and gentle Gueſt
    To viſit thee intendeth :
All that Heaven hath fair and beſt,
    To greet thee condeſcendeth.

He, Whoſe Preſence e'er imparts
    A Joy which paſſeth meaſure,
He, Whoſe Friendſhip on all hearts
    Beſtoweth boundleſs pleaſure,
Would poſſeſs this breaſt of thine,
    With Thee His Sojourn making,
With thee at thy Board recline,
    With Thee His Supper taking.

Ariſe, and run to meet Thy LORD,
    E'en now His Steps are near thee ;
Thine heart a hallowed ſhrine afford
    For Him to dwell and cheer thee ;
Oh, hold Him faſt in Thine embrace,
    Let Him go from Thee never,
Till with the fulneſs of His Grace,
    He bleſs thee, here and ever.

The Ceaseless Intercession of Christ.

This MAN hath an unchangeable Priesthood . . . seeing
He ever liveth to make Intercession for them.

ATHER of Love, Who didſt not ſpare
　　For us Thine Only SON,
　Oh, look on Him, and hear the prayer
　　Of Thy poor ſuppliant one—

Behold His pierced Hands and Feet,
　　Pleading for us e'en now ;
Behold that wounded Heart ſo ſweet ;
　　Behold, upon His Brow

The traces of the thorny Crown ;
　　Behold the ſtripes He bore ;
By theſe, He claims us for His Own—
　　His Own, for evermore.

Oh, look on Him, and let the Cry
　　Of this our Brother's BLOOD,
Who, Guiltleſs, for our guilt did die,
　　Aſcend to Thee our GOD.

It ſues for Pardon and for Peace
　　For each unworthy Son,
For Mercy, and reſtoring Grace—
　　Wilt Thou refuſe the Boon ?

Wilt Thou refuse His Love, His Toil,
   The one Reward they crave?
Shall His moſt deadly foe deſpoil
   The Souls He died to ſave?

Far be it from Thee, FATHER Sweet:
   Nor wilt Thou turn away
When by Thoſe Merits we entreat,
   When in that Name we pray;

For this is Thy Beloved SON,
   In Whom Thou art well pleaſed;
Who for the ſins that we had done
   Thine Anger juſt appeaſed.

Clothed in His Raiment we appear,
   Kneeling before His Throne,
Beſprinkled with that BLOOD ſo dear
   The Garment Thou wilt own.

And for Its ſake, the ſinner vile
   Thus made Thy wedding Gueſt
E'en ſuch an one as her, erewhile
   By ſeven fiends poſſeſſed.

No depths of ſin can drown that Love,
   No water quench its fire:
Deſponding Soul, ariſe, and prove
   Its Might, its ſtrong Deſire:

Come, yea in lowlieſt confidence,
 Approach in JESU's Name :
Greater His Love than all offence—
 FATHER, that Love we claim.

Bending before Thine Altar low,
 We offer It to Thee :
The pureſt Offering earth can know,
 Or Heaven look down to ſee.

FATHER of Mercies, we draw near
 In Thy Beloved SON :
Oh, look on Him, and hear the prayer
 Of Thy poor ſuppliant one.

𝕿𝖍𝖊 𝕱𝖔𝖚𝖓𝖙𝖆𝖎𝖓 𝖔𝖕𝖊𝖓𝖊𝖉 𝖋𝖔𝖗 𝕾𝖎𝖓.

*In that day there ſhall be a Fountain opened for ſin and
for uncleanneſs.*

THERE is a Fountain filled with BLOOD,
 Drawn from IMMANUEL's Veins,
And ſinners plunged beneath that Flood
 Loſe all their guilty ſtains.
No taint of Adam's fallen race,
 No blot of crimſon dye,
Can paſs uncleanſed that Fount of Grace,
 Or JESU's Love defy.

JESUS, the FATHER'S only SON,
   The Heaven's Eternal King,
Our nature took, our pardon won,
   And drew from Death his ſting.
For ever from His wounded Side
   Flow Streams of endleſs Life,
And thence, with holy Strength ſupplied,
   We conquer in the ſtrife.

Dear Dying LAMB, Thy Precious BLOOD
   Shall never loſe Its Power,
Till all the ranſomed Church of GOD
   Are ſaved for evermore.
For this Thy vaſt redeeming Love,
   Moſt Holy TRINITY,
From Saints on earth and Saints above
   Eternal praiſe to Thee.

Prayer and Sacrifice.

*In every place Incenſe ſhall be offered unto Me, and a
pure Offering.*
We have an Altar.

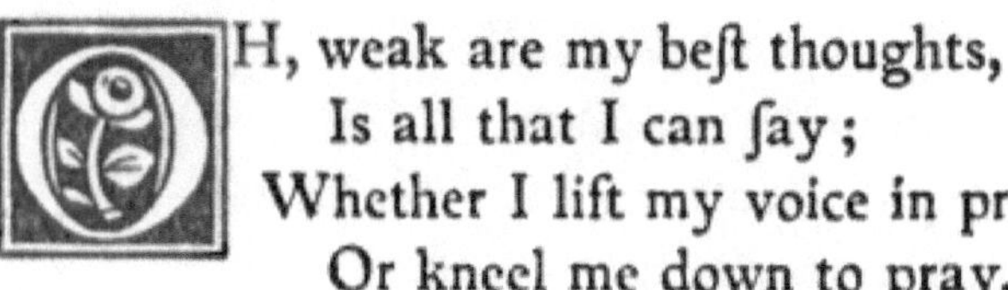

H, weak are my beſt thoughts, and poor
   Is all that I can ſay;
Whether I lift my voice in praiſe,
   Or kneel me down to pray.

Wherefore I thank Thee, Gracious LORD,
　　Whoſe Love provides for me
A higher, and more perfect way
　　Of drawing nigh to Thee—

The Way of Sacrifice—ordained
　　When earth was in its prime,
Uſed by the hoary Patriarchs
　　All through the olden time.

To Iſrael's Children in the Law
　　Of trembling Sinai given ;
To us in later days confirmed
　　By CHRIST Himſelf from Heaven.

O ſweet ecſtatic thought, 'tis mine
　　To offer, as of yore,
A Sacrifice, and One in Power
　　Excelling all before.

For me, upon an Altar fair,
　　Is pleaded, day by day,
The BODY and the BLOOD of Him
　　Whom Heaven and earth obey.

For me is immolated ſtill,
　　Again and yet again,
In the pure Hoſt, the Very LAMB
　　On Calvary's Altar ſlain.

And as the ſcarcely buoyant plank,
   Knit in the veſſel's ſide,
With eaſe careers acroſs the waves
   O'er leagues of ocean wide,

So, too, though weak my prayer, O LORD,
   Though poor my praiſes be,
Yet, knit with this high Sacrifice,
   They win their way to Thee.

𝕬n 𝕬ncient 𝕳ymn of the xv. Century.

Electum O Frumentum.

HOLY Wheat elected,
   When wilt Thou come to me ?
Stay of my heart dejected,
   It would Thy Temple be.
E'en as Thy Will hath ſpoken
It lies beneath Thee broken ;
Oh, when, oh, when the token
   That it hath Thee ?

Keen be my faith and ſteady,
   Far be all ſtain of ſin ;
O GOD, my heart is ready,
   O JESU, enter in.
Shall my love fail ? Oh, never ;
This be my one endeavour,
Here be Thy reſt for ever,
   Grant I may win.

Eucharistic Precept and Prayer.

This do in Remembrance of Me.
Lord, remember me when Thou comeſt into Thy Kingdom.

UNTO Thy Feaſt with heart deep huſhed,
    And lowly bended knee,
    As Thou commandedſt, Bleſſed Lord,
    I come, remembering Thee.

With thankfulneſs that weeps its joy,
    I liſten tremblingly,
Unto the Words of Love Divine—
    My Blood was ſhed for thee,

My Body given—Jesu, Lord,
    Through all I fly to Thee ;
In life, in death, at every hour
    Do Thou remember me.

Grant Thou me Food to ſtay my Soul,
    That I in Thee may live ;
Till I have left this mortal ſtrife
    Vouchſafe that Food to give.

When fought the fight, and kept the faith,
    Death comes to ſet me free,
Receive me, Jesu, let me in;
    In Love remember me.

A Hymn of Angelus, of the xvii. Century.

Liebe die du mich so milde.

LOVE, Who formedſt me to wear
    The Image of Thy GODHEAD here ;
Who ſoughteſt me with tender care
    Through all my wanderings wild and
        drear ;
    O Love, I give myſelf to Thee,
    Thine ever, only Thine to be.

O Love, Who ere life's earlieſt dawn
    Thy choice on me hath gently laid ;
O Love, Who here as MAN waſt born,
    And wholly like to us waſt made ;
    O Love, I give myſelf to Thee,
    Thine ever, only Thine to be.

O Love, Who once in time waſt ſlain,
    Pierced through and through with bitter woe ;
O Love, Who wreſtling thus didſt gain,
    That we eternal Joy might know ;
    O Love, I give myſelf to Thee,
    Thine ever, only Thine to be.

O Love, of Whom is Truth and Light,
    The WORD and SPIRIT, Life and Power,

Whoſe Heart was bared to them that ſmite,
 To ſhield us in our trial hour;
  O Love, I give myſelf to Thee,
  Thine ever, only Thine to be.

O Love, Who thus haſt bound me faſt
 Beneath that gentle Yoke of Thine;
Love, Who haſt conquered me at laſt,
 And wrapt away this heart of mine;
  O Love, I give myſelf to Thee,
  Thine ever, only Thine to be.

O Love, Who loveſt me for aye,
 Who for my Soul doſt ever plead;
O Love, Who didſt my Ranſom pay,
 Whoſe Power ſufficeth in my ſtead;
  O Love, I give myſelf to Thee,
  Thine ever, only Thine to be.

O Love, Who once ſhalt bid me riſe,
 From out this dying life of ours;
O Love, Who once o'er yonder ſkies,
 Shall ſet me in the fadeleſs bowers;
  O Love, I give myſelf to Thee,
  Thine ever, only Thine to be.

The Penitent's Soliloquy and Petition before Holy Communion.

*Come unto Me, all that travail and are heavy laden,
and I will refreſh you.*

I COME, O Lord, to Thee:
In ſad and grievous thought, I hear
Thy Call;
And I muſt come, or elſe from Thee I
fall
Deeper in miſery.

I have not ſought Thy Face:
And yet, Thou biddeſt me to taſte Thy Love,
Drawing my faithleſs heart to things above,
By Thy redeeming Grace.

Shame wraps my heart around,
Like morning's gloom upon the mountains ſpread;
Indignant memory—Avenger dread—
Deepens each reſtleſs wound:

Yet muſt I come to Thee:
Thou haſt the Words of Life, and Thou alone;
Thou ſitt'ſt upon the Mediator's Throne;
Where ſhould a ſinner flee?

> Nor Saints', nor Angels' will
> Could lift the burden from this wounded breaſt;
> Weary, I come to Thee, and Thou wilt give me
> reſt,
> Thou wilt Thy Words fulfil.

> I come to Thee : ſince all
> To Faith is poſſible, in Faith I come,
> As blind, and deaf, and maimed, and halt, and
> dumb;
> Before Thy Feet I fall.

> Whom didſt Thou turn away?
> From what diſtreſs was hid Thy pitying Eye?
> What cold rebuke e'er checked the ſinner's cry?
> Can I unheeded pray?

> SAVIOUR, oh, come, and ſave :
> Speak but the Word; Thy Servant ſhall be whole:
> Turn, LORD, and look on me; quicken my Soul
> Out of this living grave.

> For Thou art here moſt nigh :
> Strength in this Bread, Refreſhment in this Wine
> Lie hid; in earthly things Thy Power Divine,
> My ſins to crucify.

> Enter my opening heart :
> Fill it with Love, and Peace, and Light from
> Heaven;
> Give me Thyſelf, for all in Thee is given :
> Come, never to depart.

Corpus Christi.

Lo, I am with you alway, even unto the end of the world.

REJOICE, ye Angels, and thou Church
  This day triumphant here below;
He cometh, in meekeſt Emblem clad,
  Himſelf He cometh to beſtow.
That BODY which thou gaveſt, O Earth,
  He giveth back—that FLESH, that BLOOD,
Born of the Altar's myſtic birth,
  At once thy Worſhip and thy Food.

He, Who of old on Calvary bled,
  On all thine Altars lies to-day
A bloodleſs Sacrifice, but dread,
  The LAMB in Heaven adored for aye.
His GODHEAD on the Croſs He veiled,
  His MANHOOD here He veileth too;
But Faith has eagle eyes unſcaled,
  And Love to Him ſhe loves is true.

" I will not leave you orphans. Lo,
  While laſts the world with you am I."
SAVIOUR, we ſee Thee not, but know,
  With burning hearts, that Thou art nigh.

He comes. Blue Heaven, thine incenſe breathe
  O'er all the conſecrated ſod ;
And thou, O Earth, with flowers enwreathe
  The ſteps of thine Advancing GOD.

An Invitation to the Holy Communion.

Kommt herein, ihr lieben Glieder.

FRIENDS in JESUS, now draw near,
  Brothers, ſiſters, enter here ;
  Filled with humble, glad emotion,
  Bowed in lowly, deep devotion :
Come, approach the ſacred Board,
'Tis the Supper of the LORD ;
Where the choiceſt things of Heaven
From His loving Heart are given.

He, Who, leaving Throne and Crown,
To our fallen world came down,
All our wants and woes to ſhare,
All our ſins and griefs to bear ;
He, Who journeyed weary years
In the land of toil and tears,
Onward to the Croſs and Grave
Haſtening, the loſt to ſave ;

He deviſed this Feaſt of Love,
Thus the coldeſt heart to move,

Thus to bring Himſelf more near,
Thus to make Himſelf more dear :
On the ſacred Symbols feaſting,
All the Love of JESUS taſting,
All the SPIRIT's Grace and Power,
Oh, the ſweetneſs of the hour.

Who can tell the joy, the bliſs,
Of Communion ſuch as this ;
Sink, my Soul, in deep proſtration,
Lowly, fervent adoration ;
Earth-bound hearts, at length ariſe ;
Reaſon, ſoar beyond the ſkies ;
At Thine Altar, LORD, we bend,
Let the fire from Heaven deſcend.

Huſh your anthems, Cherubim ;
Stand aſtoniſhed, Seraphim ;
Men on earth, your brothers lowly,
Dare to join your " Holy, Holy."
LORD, may Grace imparted here
In our future lives appear :
Theſe have been—let others ſay—
At the gates of Heaven to-day.

A Prayer before Holy Communion, of the xv. Century.

Salve! Suavis et Formose.

SWEET and Beauteous, hail to Thee!
God, Who so hast loved me,
Jesu Gentle, Jesu Dear,
When I stand Thine Altar near,
   Grant me to be ranked among
   Those elect who round Thee throng,
      Fill me with Thy fullest Grace.

Hail! O Christ, Thou Saviour Blest,
Only Hope of Souls distressed,
Hear, oh, hear me, as I pray,
Purge, O Lord, my guilt away;
   And, to baffle Satan's art,
   Give me saintliness of heart,
      Every evil from me chase.

Hail to Thee! O Royal Head,
Which beneath the thorns hast bled,
Marked with spitting and with Gore,
Whence the Hair Thy foemen tore;
   Bow down, Lord, Thyself, and hear,
   To Thy servant's prayer give ear,
      Hearken, O Redeemer mild.

Hail to Thee! my Saviour's Side,
Whence poured forth the mingled Tide,
When the Blood and Water flowed
Where the Spear had made a road;
  In that Fountain waſh me, Lord,
  Throughly cleanſe the guilt abhorred
    Of my Soul by ſin defiled.

Hail! O Stream, when waſhed by Thee,
All the world from ſtain is free,
From a ſpotleſs Heart and pure
Thou haſt flowed to work our cure:
  May the voice of ſaintly prayer
  Riſe to Christ for me, who dare
    Of this Cup to drink to-day.

Hail! O Son of God moſt High,
What I longed for, now have I;
Through this precious Gift, once more,
When this life is paſt and o'er,
  Guard me from my cruel foe,
  Grant me, Lord, Thy Face to know,
    And to dwell with Thee for aye.

Our Daily Bread.

Give us this day our daily Bread.

GIVE us our daily Bread,
 O God, the Bread of ſtrength ;
For we have learnt to know
 How weak we are at length :
As children we are weak,
 As children muſt be fed ;
Give us Thy Grace, O Lord,
 To be our daily Bread.

Give us our daily Bread,
 The bitter bread of grief :
We ſought earth's poiſoned feaſts
 For pleaſure and relief ;
We ſought her deadly fruits,
 But now, O God, inſtead,
We aſk Thy healing Grief
 To be our daily Bread.

Give us our daily Bread
 To cheer our fainting Soul ;
The Feaſt of Comfort, Lord,
 And Peace, to make us whole ;
For we are ſick of tears,
 The uſeleſs tears we ſhed ;
Now give us Comfort, Lord,
 To be our daily Bread.

Give us our daily Bread,
  The Bread of Angels, Lord,
By us, ſo many times,
  Broken, betrayed, adored;
His Body and His Blood,
  The Feaſt that Jesus ſpread;
Give Him—our Life, our All—
  To be our daily Bread.

𝔏atus 𝔖albatoris.

*One of the ſoldiers with a ſpear pierced His Side, and
forthwith came thereout Blood and Water.*

HERE is an everlaſting Home,
  Where contrite Souls may hide;
Where death and danger dare not come—
  The Saviour's Side.

It was a cleft of matchleſs Love,
  Opened when He had died,
When Mercy hailed in worlds above
  That wounded Side.

Hail! Rock of Ages, pierced for me,
  The grave of all my pride;
Hope, Peace, and Heaven, are all in Thee,
  Thy ſheltering Side.

There iſſued forth the double Flood,
  The ſin-atoning Tide,

In ſtreams of Water and of BLOOD,
    From that dear Side.

There is the only Fount of Bliſs,
    In joy and ſorrow tried ;
No refuge for the heart like this,
    A SAVIOUR's Side.

Thither the Church, through all her days,
    Points as a faithful guide,
And celebrates with ceaſeleſs praiſe,
    That ſpear-pierced Side.

Kyrie Eleiſon.

HERR JESU CHRISTE, *mein getreuer Hirte.*

LORD JESUS CHRIST, my faithful Shep-
    herd, hear ;
    Feed me with Thy Grace, draw inly
    near ;
By Thee redeem'd, in Thee alone I live,
All I need 'tis Thou canſt give :
        Kyrie Eleiſon.

Ah, LORD, Thy timid ſheep now feed
With joy upon Thy Heavenly mead,
Lead us to the cryſtal River
Whence our life is flowing ever :
        Kyrie Eleiſon.

For Thou art calling all the toil-oppreſſed,
All the weary to Thy Reſt;
   The pardon of their ſins is here beſtow'd,
   Thou doſt free them from their load:
                Kyrie Eleiſon.

Ah, come, Thyſelf put forth Thine Hand,
Unbind this heavy iron band,
   Set me from my ſorrows free,
   Give me ſtrength to follow Thee:
                Kyrie Eleiſon.

Thou fain wouldſt heart and Soul to Thee incline,
Take me from myſelf and make me Thine;
   Thou art the Vine and I the branch, oh, grant
   I may grow in Thee a living plant:
                Kyrie Eleiſon.

For nought but ſin I find in me,
Yet are they done away in Thee;
   Mine are anguiſh, fear, unreſt,
   But in Thee, LORD, I am bleſt:
                Kyrie Eleiſon.

An Ode of S. John Damascene, of the viii. Century.

Μέγα τὸ Μυστήριον.

CHRIST, we turn our eyes to Thee,
And this mighty Myſtery:
Habakkuk exclaimed of old,
In the HOLY SPIRIT bold—
Thou ſhalt come in time appointed,
For the help of Thine Anointed.

Taſte of Myrrh He deigned to know,
Who redeemed the ſource of woe:
Now He bids all ſickneſs ceaſe
Through the Honeycomb of Peace;
And to this world deigns to give
That ſweet Fruit by which we live.

Patient LORD, with loving Eye
Thou inviteſt Thomas nigh,
Showing of that wounded Side;
While the world is certified
How the third day, from the Grave,
JESUS CHRIST aroſe to ſave.

Bleſt, O Didymus, the tongue
Where that firſt Confeſſion hung,
Firſt the SAVIOUR to proclaim,
Firſt the LORD of Life to name;
Such the Graces it ſupplied—
That dear touch of JESU's Side.

The Cross the Anticipation of the Altar.

*He was wounded for our transgressions; He was bruised
for our iniquities.*

TALK not of Bread; the Soul, entranced, but eyes
    That Heavenly FORM, so buffeted and bruised:
Talk not of Wine; the Soul, entranced, descries
    That Brow, that Side, with Healing BLOOD suffused:
Nor tell me of a consecrated Board;
    Hence with the wings of wafting Faith I rove;
On Golgotha, before th' Expiring LORD,
    I bend in grief, astonishment, and love.

Sweet is the liquid grape to him that glows
    With gasping thirst, or bread to starved distress;
But sweeter far a SAVIOUR's Death to those
    Who thirst and hunger after Righteousness.
Oh, as the branch is nourished by the Vine—
    Thou, SAVIOUR, art the Vine, the branches we—
Still may our Spirits, in this mystic Wine,
    Drink life, health, beauty, joy, festivity.

A Meditation on the Holy Eucharist.

So man did eat Angels' Food; for He sent them
Meat enough.

JESU, we laud and worſhip Thee,
The veiled Incarnate DEITY;
Since ſinful man eats Angels' Food—
The Bread of Life, the Precious BLOOD.

Oft as we ſeek Thine Altar-Throne,
Help every Soul in ſuppliant tone,
As Love's own voice comes whiſpering by,
To aſk with tears—LORD, is it I?

LORD, is it I, who doubt if Thou
Art really Preſent with us now,
Preſent to calm each aching breaſt,
To give the heavy laden reſt?

LORD, is it I, who turn away,
And go like Judas to betray,
As if no Paſchal BLOOD had gleamed
On lips, which Grace has once redeemed?

JESU, what Love can Thine tranſcend,
Love without meaſure, time, or end;
Which gives to thoſe who ſeek Thy Feet,
Thy BLOOD to drink, Thy FLESH to eat?

Oh, Glory, that no tongue can tell,
Oh, Preſence moſt ineffable,
Hidden in Forms of Bread and Wine,
Faith now adores her LORD Divine.

Yes, ſpotleſs Victim, ſinleſs Prieſt,
We hail Thee in this awful Feaſt ;
And pray through It our Souls uplift
To Thee, the Giver and the Gift.

In hours of woe, in time of wealth,
Be this ſweet Food the Spirit's health—
Till in this Strength we reach our home,
Till to the Mount of GOD we come.

There we ſhall ſee, unveiled at laſt,
When Holy Sacraments are paſt,
The Preſence which on earth we own,
And know even as we are known.

JESU, all laud and praiſe to Thee,
At this high Feaſt our prayer ſhall be
That we, who hymn this mighty Grace,
In Heaven may ſee Thee Face to face.

An Ancient Canticle.

Uncta Crux DEI CRUORE.

WITH the Precious BLOOD anointed,
   Thee we hail, O holieſt Tree!
Life at thy bleſt touch returning
   Owns thy wondrous potency:
Such thy glory, ſuch thy virtue
   Since our SAVIOUR hung on thee.

Fount of univerſal Bleſſing
   From the Wounds of JESUS poured,
Let the wounded gaze upon thee
   And their healing is aſſured;
Only let them look, believing,
   They ſhall prove their LORD's dear Word.

Holy Croſs, thou Seat of Judgment,
   Where the Juſt One ſat enthroned,
To pronounce the righteous Sentence,
   Yet His righteous Ire diſowned
When He bare the Wood of healing,
   Who the Rod of vengeance owned.

Thou in Whom all things are holy,
   Only ſpring of Sanɛtity,

Though our ſins be dark and fearful
    Thou canſt waſh their ſtain away;
Let Thy healing dews refreſh us
    In our laſt ſharp agony.

To the FATHER, the Creator,
    Everlaſting Glory be;
To the SON, Who willed to ſuffer
    That the captive might go free;
To the SPIRIT, Who doth guide us
    Into Peace and Sanctity.

PART II.

THE OBLATION.

The Offering of the New Law, the One
Oblation once Offered.

Sacrifice and Offering Thou wouldeſt not, but a BODY
haſt Thou prepared Me.

NCE I thought to ſit ſo high
In the Palace of the ſky;
Now, I thank GOD for His Grace,
If I may fill the loweſt place.

Once I thought to ſcale ſo ſoon
Heights above the changing moon;
Now, I thank GOD for delay—
To-day, it yet is called to-day.

While I ſtumble, halt and blind,
Lo! He waiteth to be kind;
Bleſs me ſoon, or bleſs me ſlow,
Except He bleſs, I let not go.

Once for earth I laid my plan,
Once I leaned on ſtrength of man,
When my hope was ſwept aſide,
I ſtayed my broken heart on pride:

Broken reed hath pierced my hand;
Fell my houſe I built on ſand;
Roofleſs, wounded, maimed by ſin,
Fightings without and fears within:

Yet, a tree, He feeds my root;
Yet, a branch, He prunes for fruit;
Yet, a ſheep, theſe eves and morns,
He ſeeks for me among the thorns.

With Thine Image ſtamped of old,
Find Thy coin more choice than gold;
Known to Thee by name, recall
To Thee Thy home-ſick prodigal.

Sacrifice and Offering
None there is that I can bring;
None, ſave what is Thine alone:
I bring Thee, LORD, but of Thine Own—

Broken BODY, BLOOD Outpoured,
Theſe I bring, my GOD, my LORD;
Wine of Life, and Living Bread,
With theſe for me Thy Board is ſpread.

The Oblation.

A Sacrifice acceptable, well-pleasing to God.

The Lamb *slain from the foundation of the world.*

YEA, Thou waſt once a Victim ſlain,
Thy Manhood in the atoning pain
Was offered once, and ne'er again.

But, Lord, in their immortal worth,
Thy Flesh and Blood are ſtill ſet forth
Before God's Throne, in Heaven and earth.

For, Preſent whereſoe'er they be,
By Nature's rule or Myſtery,
We have Thy Sacrifice and Thee.

And Preſent truly and indeed,
In Sacrament our Souls to feed,
That Flesh and Blood are ſtrong to plead.

For in Them never fails nor dies
The Might of Thy dread Sacrifice
That ſtands before the Father's Eyes.

And thus on lowlieſt Altar floor,
E'en as within the eternal door,
They ſhow Thy Paſſion evermore.

O Thou, Whoſe Love can thus combine
The earthly with the Heavenly ſhrine,
Let this pure Offering keep us Thine.

A Hymn of S. Andrew of Crete, of the viii. Century.

Τὸ μέγα Μυστήριον.

OH, the Myſtery, paſſing wonder,
    When reclining at the Board,
Eat—Thou ſaidſt to Thy Diſciples—
    That true Bread with quickening
        ſtored ;
Drink in faith the healing Chalice,
    From a Dying GOD outpoured.

Then the glorious upper Chamber
    A celeſtial Tent was made,
When the Bloodleſs Rite wás offered,
    And the Soul's true ſervice paid,
And the table of the feaſters
    As an Altar ſtood diſplayed.

CHRIST is now our mighty Paſcha,
    Eaten for our myſtic Bread ;
As a Lamb led out to ſlaughter,
    And for this world offerèd ;
Take we of His Broken BODY,
    Drink we of the BLOOD He ſhed.

To the Twelve ſpake Truth eternal,
    To the branches ſpake the Vine—

Never more from this day forward
  Shall I taſte again this Wine,
Till I drink it in the Kingdom
  Of My FATHER, and with Mine.

Thou haſt ſtretched thoſe hands for ſilver
  That had held th' immortal Food;
With thoſe lips that late had taſted
  Of the BODY and the BLOOD,
Thou haſt given the kiſs, O Judas;
  Thou haſt heard the Woe beſtowed.

CHRIST to all the world gives Banquet
  On that moſt Celeſtial Meat;
Him, albeit with lips all earthly,
  Yet with holy hearts we greet,
Him the ſacrificial Paſcha,
  Prieſt and Victim all complete.

A Colloquy between the Diſciple and the Divine Maſter.

In my trouble, I will call upon the LORD; ſo ſhall He hear my voice out of His holy Temple.

Peccator ad CHRISTUM.

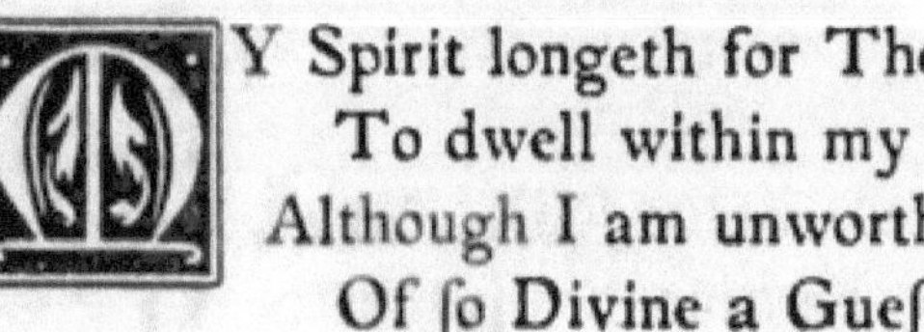

Y Spirit longeth for Thee
  To dwell within my breaſt;
Although I am unworthy
  Of ſo Divine a Gueſt:

Of ſo Divine a Gueſt,
  Unworthy though I be ;
Yet hath my heart no reſt
  Until it come to Thee :

Until it come to Thee,
  In vain I look around ;
In all that I can ſee,
  No reſt is to be found :

No reſt is to be found,
  But in Thy bleeding Love ;
Oh, let my wiſh be crowned,
  And ſend it from above.

CHRISTUS *ad Peccatorem.*

Cheer up, deſponding Soul,
  Thy longing pleaſed I ſee ;
'Tis part of that great whole,
  Wherewith I longed for thee :

Wherewith I longed for thee,
  And left My FATHER's Throne,
From death to ſet thee free,
  And claim thee for My Own :

To claim thee for My Own,
  I ſuffered on the Croſs ;
Oh, were My Love but known,
  All elſe would be as droſs :

All elſe would be as droſs,
    And Souls, through Grace Divine,
Would count their gains but loſs,
    To live for ever Mine.

A Veſper Hymn of S. Thomas Aquinas, of the xiii. Century.

Sacris Solemniis junƈta ſint gaudia.

LET this our ſolemn Feaſt
    With holy joys be crowned,
And from each loving breaſt
    The voice of gladneſs ſound;
Let ancient things depart,
    And all be new around,
In every aƈt and voice and heart.

Remember we that Eve,
    That Supper laſt and dread,
When CHRIST, as we believe,
    The Lamb and leavenleſs Bread
Unto His Brethren brought;
    And thus the Law obeyed,
Of old time to the Fathers taught.

But when the Law's repaſt
    Was o'er, the Type complete,
To His Diſciples laſt
    The LORD His FLESH to eat,

The Whole to all, no leſs
   The Whole to each, doth meet,
With His Own Hand, as we confeſs.

He gave the weak and frail,
   His BODY for their Food ;
The ſad, for their regale,
   The Chalice of His BLOOD ;
And ſaid—Take ye of This,
   My Cup with Life imbued ;
Oh, drink ye all this Draught of Bliſs.

.That Sacrifice ſo He
   To inſtitute did will,
And by a ſure Decree
   That Office to fulfil,
To Prieſts alone confide,
   To whom pertaineth ſtill
To take, and to the reſt divide.

Lo ! Angels' Bread is made
   The Bread of mortal man ;
Shows forth this Heavenly Bread
   The end which Types began ;
Oh, wondrous boon indeed,
   Upon his LORD now can
A poor and humble ſervant feed.

Thee, DEITY TRIUNE
   Yet ONE, we meekly pray,

Oh, viſit us right ſoon,
As we our homage pay;
And in Thy Footſteps bright,
Conduct us on our way,
To where Thou dwell'ſt in cloudleſs Light.

Chriſtmas Midnight Celebration of the Holy Euchariſt.

Glory to GOD *in the Higheſt, and on earth Peace, Good-will towards men.*

ALLELUIA! LORD moſt Holy,
In Thy Manger-throne we hail
Thee;
Alleluia! Meek and Lowly,
Never ſhall our worſhip fail Thee.

Alleluia! choirs of Angels
Sing at midnight-hour Thy Glory,
To the watchful ſhepherds telling
From the ſkies Thy natal ſtory.

Alleluia! CHILD of Mary,
Low the ſhepherds bend before Thee;
Alleluia! eaſtern Monarchs
With their coſtlieſt gifts adore Thee.

Alleluia! ſtill unended
Rings the Angel-note above;

From our Altars ſweetly blending
  Echoes earth's reſponſe of love.

Alleluia ! ſhine the tapers,
  Gleams the holly's burniſhed ſpray ;
Alleluia ! chant the Credo,
  CHRIST, we welcome Thee to-day.

Alleluia ! LORD moſt Mighty,
  Come upon our ſhrines to dwell ;
Alleluia ! Deareſt JESUS ;
  Hark, it ſounds—the ſanctus-bell.

Down in adoration falling,
  Hail ! ſweet Sacrament Divine ;
Hail ! to Thee our Souls are calling,
  Thou art ours, and we are Thine.

𝕸𝖎𝖉𝖓𝖎𝖌𝖍𝖙 𝕮𝖍𝖗𝖎𝖘𝖙𝖒𝖆𝖘 𝕮𝖔𝖒𝖒𝖚𝖓𝖎𝖔𝖓.

He came unto His Own, and His Own received Him not.

OUT on the world, unheeded, came there
      One at midnight hour,
    A lowly Maid His Mother, and a
      Manger-ſtall His bed ;
Out on the cold, cold winter, when the ſnow lay
    on the ground,
He came a Tender INFANT to Bethlehem's humble
    ſhed.

Out on the world, unheeded—for none knew that
　　He was GOD,
Save His Parents, and the ſhepherds, and the
　　ſtrangers from afar ;
Theſe were His ſole adorers—theſe the courtiers
　　of the King,
The world ſaw not the riſing of the bright and
　　morning Star.

Out on the world, forſaken, poor He comes to ſin-
　　ners ſtill,
When ſtorms are raging fiercely, and 'tis night
　　becauſe of ſin ;
Out on the cold, cold winter—to their thankleſs
　　hearts He comes,
And they turn their faces from Him, and will not
　　take Him in.

Out on the world, neglected—careleſs Chriſtians
　　love Him not
While on our Altars dwelling, veiled in Myſtery
　　moſt high ;
Unbelieving they reject Him—they will not own
　　their LORD,
Out on the cold, cold winter—for they paſs un-
　　mindful by.

Out on the world, forſaken—but the faithful take
　　Him in,
As to her Breaſt did Mary on that firſt glad
　　Chriſtmas night ;

And where'er the red lamp's gleaming tells of the
    Hidden GOD,
They bend the knee and worſhip Him, Who is the
    Light of light.

And every lowly boſom which receives Him
    tenderly
He ſtrengthens with His Preſence, and His Bleſ-
    ſing comfort brings ;
What joy to that poor dwelling when the LORD
    of Glory comes—
Another Bethlehem's Manger to enthrone the
    King of kings.

Such be my heart, Dear JESUS, this bleſſed Chriſt-
    mas morn ;
Cold, cold the world unheeding, but my Gueſt
    vouchſafe to be ;
Though mean and poor the dwelling, true my
    heart's glad welcome is,
And this my prayer unceaſing—Stay Thou ever-
    more with me.

Out on the world, forſaken—Oh, regard Thy
    Children's love—
Our tears be Reparation for the ſlights upon
    Thee thrown ;
May the Church's great Thankſgiving, this Holy
    Sacrifice,
Avail for all the thankleſs, and for all our ſins
    atone.

Alleluia ! Alleluia ! Sing every tongue with joy ;
He comes to dwell amongſt us, our ſweet Sacra-
　　mental King ;
Raiſe up to Heaven your anthems, and the frag-
　　rant cenſers wave,
Telling out to every people this great and wondrous
　　thing.

Alleluia ! Alleluia ! Till Death our voices huſh,
Till we join the Church Triumphant, and reach
　　the Fount of Grace ;
There no more the hidden Preſence, nor Eu-
　　chariſtic Rite,
But the Bridegroom's Marriage Supper, and to
　　ſee Him Face to face.

A Carol for Christmas-tide.

Behold, the BRIDEGROOM *cometh ; go ye out to
meet Him.*

NOW lift the Carol, men and maids,
　　Now make exultant ſinging,
This day the Well of Life firſt ſprang—
　　Who ſhall declare its ſpringing ?
It is the Birthday of our Peace ;
　　This day for man, the weary,
The Everlaſting SON of GOD
　　Was born of Bleſſèd Mary.

He was not born in such sweet days
  As we of yore remember;
It was not sunny summer-time,
  Oh, it was bleak December:
Over our heads the sun is bright,
  Beneath the snow falls slacken,
So, unto this dark wintry world
  He came, the dead to quicken.

He did not bring a royal train,
  A host no man could number;
Nor lay begirt by damask folds,
  Nor lulled by harp to slumber;
Oh, He was wrapped in swathing bands
  Whose Might o'erspans the Heaven,
And a poor trough, whence oxen fed,
  For His first rest was given.

But there were shepherds at the fold
  Who heard the wondrous tiding,
How there was joy in Heav'n that night
  For peace on earth abiding.
They went in haste to Bethlehem,
  And saw, and told the story
Of CHRIST, the LORD, a Little CHILD,
  And Angels singing—Glory.

He lies not in the manger now—
  Far o'er the sapphire portal
At the Right Hand of Pow'r He sits,
  Who was this day made mortal:

All in the higheſt, holieſt Place,
  Where there may dwell none other,
There our own Manhood ſits enthroned,
  There is our Elder Brother.

He has gone up into His Home—
  Will there be no returning
Until His awful Sign is ſeen,
  And Heaven and earth are burning?
O Brother, He will come : He came
  Once in our nature Lowly ;
But now in lowlier Wine and Bread
  We take the Ever-holy.

Lo! He is coming ; lo! the Bride
  Her pureſt white is wearing ;
Lo! the twin tapers ſhed their gleam,
  The Two-fold CHRIST declaring ;
And lo! the Prieſt, His Miniſter,
  Stands between earth and Heaven
To ſpeak the ancient Law anew
  Before its end be given.

The Birthday of our GOD and King—
  Lo! we are called to greet Him ;
The everlaſting Bridegroom comes,
  Oh, go ye out to meet Him.
This is the end of all below,
  The crown of Love's beſt ſtory ;
CHRIST ſtands and knocks—oh, happy Souls,
  Receive the King of Glory.

An Ancient Hymn for Maundy Thursday: from the German.

Israel doth not know, My people do not consider.

IN those dark hours of bitter Woe,
    When depths of Agony
  Bound Me to dust, I bade It flow—
    My BLOOD, in Streams for thee:
I stood alone, My Hands were bound;
    Beneath the scourge I stood;
From their long furrows to the ground
    Fast fell the Holy BLOOD.
My Child, oh, this was all for Thee;
Oh, hast Thou ever thought of Me?

They put on Me a Robe of scorn,
    Bade thorns My Crown to be;
I gladly bore it, could have borne
    More still for love of thee;
They gave Me then the Cross to bear,
    And many a word was said
Against My holy Name, but ne'er—
    Love from My Heart ne'er fled.
My Child, oh, this was all for Thee;
Oh, hast thou ever thought of Me?

Behold Me lifted up on high,
    Praying midst all My Woe,

With parched Lip and clofing Eye,
  My FATHER for each foe,
And then, with Heart-wrung Wail and Groan—
  My GOD, My GOD—I faid;
It feemed that I was left alone,
  And My true Comfort fled.
My Child, oh, this was all for Thee;
Oh, haft thou ever thought of Me?

The Gentile's fpear hath pierced My Side;
  Lo! from My Heart within
Water and BLOOD, a pricelefs Tide,
  Flow forth to cleanfe from fin.
Have I left any thing undone,
  So thou by it might'ft be
Brought back, My loft, My loved One?
  Have I not died for thee?
My Child, oh, this was all for Thee;
Oh, haft thou ever thought of Me?

For Thee I was content to die,
  To fhame and anguifh moved;
And now, upon My Throne on high
  I love as then I loved;
To thee My FLESH and BLOOD are given—
  The pure Soul's myftic Food—
And thou fhalt be with Me in Heaven
  When thou haft paffed Death's flood.
My Child, oh, this was all for Thee;
Oh, haft thou ever thought of Me?

Easter Celebration of Holy Mysteries.

The LORD *is Rifen indeed.*

THOU, that on the firft of Eafters,
 Cam'ft refplendent from the Tomb,
Leaving all Thy linen Cerements
 Folded in the Cavern's gloom,
Come with Thine—All hail—to greet us,
 Come our Pafchal joy to be;
Let our Altar, clad in brightnefs,
 Yield a Throne of white for Thee.

This fhall crown the Queen of Sundays;
 Grant but this—our cup runs o'er;
Hymns that welcomed in Thine Eafter
 Made us long for this the more:
All the Pafchal Alleluias
 Craved to fee the LAMB appear;
Come the hour when Faith fhall tell us—
 He is rifen; He is here.

Thou, Whofe all-tranfcendent MANHOOD
 Knew not aught of bonds impofed,
Rifing ere the ftone was lifted,
 Paffing where the doors were clofed,
Prefent here in very Effence,
 Is there aught too hard for Thee?
Fill us with Thy Light and Sweetnefs,
 From our darknefs make us free.

AGNUS DEI, we are guilty;
  Panis Vitæ, we are faint;
But Thou didſt not riſe at Eaſter
  To be deaf to our complaint;
Come, oh, come to cleanſe and feed us,
  Breathing Peace and kindling Love,
Till Thy Paſchal Bleſſings bear us
  To the Feaſt of feaſts above.

Holy Communion on Easter Day.

Ad Regias AGNI *Dapes.*

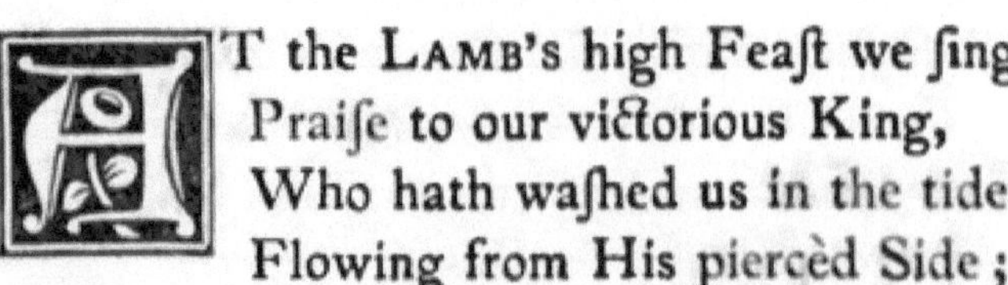

AT the LAMB's high Feaſt we ſing
  Praiſe to our victorious King,
  Who hath waſhed us in the tide
  Flowing from His piercèd Side;
Praiſe we Him Whoſe Love Divine
Gives His Sacred BLOOD for Wine,
Gives His BODY for the Feaſt,
CHRIST the Victim, CHRIST the Prieſt.

Where the Paſchal BLOOD is poured,
Death's dark angel ſheathes his ſword;
Iſrael's hoſts triumphant go
Through the wave that drowns the foe.
Praiſe we CHRIST, Whoſe BLOOD was ſhed,
Paſchal Victim, Paſchal Bread;
With ſincerity and love
Eat we Manna from above.

Mighty Victim from the ſky,
Hell's fierce powers beneath Thee lie ;
Thou haſt conquered in the fight ;
Thou haſt brought us Life and Light :
Now no more can death appal,
Now no more the grave enthral ;
Thou haſt opened Paradiſe,
And in Thee Thy Saints ſhall riſe.

Eaſter triumph, Eaſter joy,
Sin alone can this deſtroy ;
From ſin's power do Thou ſet free
Souls new-born, O LORD, in Thee.
Hymns of glory and of praiſe,
Riſen LORD, to Thee we raiſe ;
Holy FATHER, praiſe to Thee,
With the SPIRIT, ever be.

𝔈𝔞𝔰𝔱𝔢𝔯 𝔠𝔢𝔩𝔢𝔟𝔯𝔞𝔱𝔦𝔬𝔫 𝔬𝔣 𝔱𝔥𝔢 𝔅𝔩𝔢𝔰𝔰𝔢𝔡 𝔖𝔞𝔠𝔯𝔞𝔪𝔢𝔫𝔱.

Unto you it is given to know the Myſteries of the Kingdom of GOD.

THE Myſtery of Myſteries :
Now let the pure in heart draw nigh,
While every pulſe is beating high
With love and holy fear ;
For CHRIST hath riſen at break of day,
And bids us from the world away,
And haſte to meet Him here.

    The Myſtery of Myſteries :
The Angels and Archangels come
On wings of Light from out their home,
    In ranks of glory wheeling ;
Our Souls ſhall mix and blend with theirs,
In loud thank-offerings and prayers,
    Before the Altar kneeling.

    The Myſtery of Myſteries :
The Souls that ſtill in dimneſs dwell
Deep in the Church inviſible,
    From doubt and care remote,
They too ſhall keep the Feaſt to-day,
And to their cells, though far away,
    The Hymn of joy ſhall float.

    The Myſtery of Myſteries :
Oh, far and wide through all the earth,
Emotions of unwonted mirth
    And feeling ſtrange ſhall be ;
And ſecret ſounds ſhall come and go,
Harmonious, as the throbbing flow
    Of the myſterious ſea.

    The Myſtery of Myſteries :
The dead and living ſhall be one,
And thrills of fiery tranſport run
    With ſweeteſt power through all ;
For one in heart and Faith are we,
And moulded one, our Head, through Thee,
    The Body Myſtical.

   The Myſtery of Myſteries :
From eaſt to weſt the world ſhall turn,
And ſtay its buſy feet to learn
   The muſical vibration ;
While Saints and Angels high ſhall raiſe,
In one vaſt choir, the hymn to praiſe
   The Feaſt of our Salvation.

𝕿𝖍𝖊 𝕯𝖎𝖛𝖎𝖓𝖊 𝕻𝖗𝖊𝖘𝖊𝖓𝖈𝖊 ; a 𝕳𝖞𝖒𝖓 for 𝕬𝖘𝖈𝖊𝖓𝖘𝖎𝖔𝖓=𝖙𝖎𝖉𝖊.

GOD *ſitteth upon His holy Seat.*

LIFT up your ſongs, ye Angel-choirs,
   Lift up your heads, ye golden gates ;
Before your jewelled portals, lo !
   The King and LORD of Glory waits :
His Robes are dyed with royal hues,
   A purple glow proclaims the fight ;
JESUS has won the world to GOD,
   And triumphed by His Princely Might.

Hark ! Heav'n's enraptured chorus ſwells,
   To welcome back th' Eternal SON ;
While every glittering Wound ſhows forth—
   At what a coſt the ſtrife was won.
Hail ! JESUS, our aſcended King ;
   Hail ! SON of Mary, SON of GOD ;
No mind can e'en conceive Thy ſtate,
   No tongue can publiſh it abroad.

At God's Right Hand Thou doſt abide,
    The Sea of Glaſs before Thee ſpread;
And, like unto an emerald,
    The Rainbow round about Thy Head:
Yet, wondrous thought, while Jesus there
    With God the Father intercedes,
The Spotleſs Lamb for ſinners ſlain
    Still on ten thouſand Altars bleeds.

Oft as the high myſterious Words
    Are duly breathed o'er Bread and Wine,
Jesu, the God Incarnate comes
    And ſeeks His holy Altar-ſhrine—
A Myſtery too deep for ſpeech;
    The ſtarry Heavens their Lord reſtore,
And wondering Angels hover near,
    While loving, trembling hearts adore.

No longer led by ſhadowy Type
    We grope our way to Love's abode,
The Croſs marks out the narrow path,
    Thy glorious Wounds light up the road:
E'en now the eye of Faith upturned
    Beholds the golden Robe of Light,
Which wrapt Thee round when on the Mount,
    Which veils Thee ſtill from mortal's ſight.

Ah! if no outward Sign be near,
    Yet we can kneel and worſhip Thee;
Each Altar is a Glory-Throne
    Where Thou for love of us wilt be:

Thus, throned in Heaven and throned on earth,
We worſhip Thee, the Victor dread :
Thou, Who the Heaven of Heavens doſt fill,
Abide with us, O Living Bread.

Afcenfion Communion.

While they beheld, He was taken up, and a cloud
received Him out of their ſight.

BORNE on triumphal clouds
The King of Glory ſoars,
While each trained faithful heart below
In wondering love adores.

Farther and farther yet
From wiſtful gaze is drawn
The glorious car, which bears away
The Joy of hearts forlorn.

Their LORD, their Life, is gone ;
The deeps of Heaven reſume
Their wonted calm, ſerenely bright,
Forbidding thoughts of gloom.

For He will ne'er forget :
E'en in His Glory hour
He ſends the Heavenly Meſſage down
To comfort them with Power.

He hath not left His Own:
  Where Faith purges the sight,
And Love the dwelling-place prepares,
  There He abides in might.

Return into your hearts,
  And ye shall find Him there;
He hath but risen, that they may rise
  And breathe of Heaven's own air.

Yea, brightening Faith shall soar
  Beyond the clouds of earth,
And hail her LORD, in glorious chant
  Of Eucharistic mirth.

Ascended, and enthroned
  At the Right Hand above,
He re-descends, to dwell with men
  In His blest Feast of Love.

And even as He went,
  So shall he daily come
Enfolded·in mysterious Cloud,
  To make in us His home.

O SAVIOUR, cleanse our Souls
  To see, and own Thee near;
That we, with Thee, may rise and dwell
  As Thou with us art here.

The Celebration at Emmaus.

They told how He was known of them in the
Breaking of BREAD.

THEY talked of JESUS, as they went;
   And JESUS, all unknown,
  Did at their ſide Himſelf preſent,
   With Sweetneſs all His Own.
Swift, as He oped the ſacred Word,
   His Glory they diſcerned;
And ſwift, as His dear Voice they heard,
   Their hearts within them burned.

He would have left them, but that they
   With prayers His Love aſſailed—
Depart not yet; a little ſtay—
   They preſſed Him, and prevailed.
And JESUS was revealed, as there
   He bleſſed, and brake the BREAD:
But, while they marked His Heavenly air,
   The matchleſs Gueſt had fled.

And thus at times, as Chriſtians talk
   Of JESUS and His Word;
He joins two friends amidſt their walk,
   And makes, unſeen, a Third.
And oh, how ſweet their converſe flows,
   Their holy theme how clear,
How warm with Love each boſom glows,
   If JESUS be but near.

And they that woo His Viſits ſweet,
 And will not let Him go,
Oft, while His broken Bread they eat,
 His Soul-felt Preſence know.
His gathered Friends He loves to meet,
 And fill with Joy their faith,
When they with melting hearts repeat
 The Memory of His Death.

But ſuch ſweet Viſits here are brief,
 Diſpenſed from ſtage to ſtage
(A cheering and a prized relief)
 Of Faith's hard pilgrimage.
There is a ſcene when JESUS ne'er,
 Ne'er leaves his happy gueſts,
He ſpreads a ceaſeleſs Banquet there,
 And Love ſtill fires their breaſts.

The Altar of the Croſs.

Signum Crux novæ Federis.

SAFE to the haven of their reſt,
 O bleſſed Croſs, thou bear'ſt the loſt,
Sign of a Covenant new and bleſt,
 Ark of a world in tempeſt toſt.

In vain doth the Avenger raiſe,
 With angry might, his red right hand ;
Thy ſilent power his wrath allays,
 Forgotten ſinks the fiery brand.

Let him, who writhes in agony
 Becauſe the Serpent's bite was ſore,
Lift up his eyes, and gaze on thee,
 And lo! he feels the ſmart no more.

Equal with GOD, the HOLY ONE
 A Sacrifice upon thee lay,
Dear Altar, whence the Bleſſed SON
 His FATHER's Anger ſoothed away.

O holieſt, O ſweeteſt Croſs,
 Thou with the Precious BLOOD art dyed;
And all amended is our loſs,
 Since on thy boſom CHRIST hath died.

Eucharistical.

The Real Preſence.

I KNOW that Thou art here, I know
  not how,
  While others argue, I Thy Word
  adore;
Body and Soul before Thee lowly bow;
 Thy Word hath ſpoken it, I aſk no more—
Who eateth Me, the ſame ſhall live by Me—
O Soul-ſubduing Voice, O Myſtery;
 My whole heart thirſteth after Thee, LORD
  CHRIST,
Therefore I live for Thy dread Euchariſt.

The Sacrifice of the Altar.

That which He offered at the Paſchal Feaſt,
 That which He offered on the fruitful Tree,
The once-ſlain Victim, Prophet, King, and Prieſt,
 FATHER, we offer here in Myſtery;
Behold the Merits, which we could not win;
Behold His Griefs, Who bore the whole world's
 ſin;
  Behold, LORD GOD, the Face of Thine Own
   CHRIST,
  Shown forth to Thee in Thy dread Euchariſt.

The Communion of Saints.

Ye Saints of GOD, Sweet JESUS' Body glorious,
 From Abel to the babe baptized but now,
Ye that in Paradiſe take reſt victorious,
 Ye that on earth beneath the Croſs ſtill bow,
Ye lightning-viſaged hoſts Angelical,
Here at this Holy Feaſt I meet you all;
  Heaven and earth are one in Thee, LORD
   CHRIST;
  Therefore I live for Thy dread Euchariſt.

Sacramental Likeneſs.

They grow alike who dwell in love together;
 And gentle holineſs doth tame and faſhion
Tenderly, as the influence of calm weather,
 The vagrant heart which owns no law but paſſion;
And ſince for Thy dear Likeneſs, LORD, I yearn,
And, wandering ever, once again return

To dwell in Thee, and Thou in me, Lord
    Christ ;
Therefore I live for Thy dread Euchariſt.

Penitence in Communion.

Deep penitence was hers, who bathed Thy Feet
    In tears that welled from out a broken heart ;
High was her lot, when Thou didſt make her meet
    In quiet love to chooſe the better part ;
More bleſt when ſhe, unſparing and deep-loving,
Did what ſhe could, and heard Thy kind approving :
    So let me gather Grace on Grace, Lord Christ ;
    Therefore I live for Thy dread Euchariſt.

The Buſineſs of Life.

To tread the way Thy holy Feet have trod,
    To keep that flinty path and never ſtray,
To live the hidden Life with Thee in God,
    To bear the Croſs with cheerful heart alway,
Learning to live, that I may know to die,
And wait in hope Thy coming Majeſty,
    This, this is what Thou willeſt, O Lord
        Christ ;
    Therefore I live for Thy dread Euchariſt.

The Will of God.

Thy Will be mine ; for nothing will I long,
    Thy perfect Will ſhall be my only care ;

Give as Thou wilt, pain, ſickneſs, grief, or wrong,
  Chill failure, or ſucceſs more hard to bear:
But grant that ſaturate with Grace Divine,
My heart may beat in harmony with Thine;
  For Thou, O GOD, art Very MAN, LORD
    CHRIST;
  Therefore I live for Thy dread Euchariſt.

Supplication at the Altar.

Aſk; and it ſhall be given unto you,
  More than ye think, and better than ye aſk:
Seek; ye ſhall find that I am Juſt and True;
  My powerful Love ye cannot overtaſk:
Knock; and it ſhall be opened.—LORD, I knock,
I ſeek, I aſk; do Thou Thy Store unlock,
  For here Thy Store is richeſt, O LORD CHRIST;
  Therefore I live for Thy dread Euchariſt.

Dryneſs before Reception.

A weary body and an o'er-wrought brain,
  No wiſh to long for Thee, no heart to love,
In hard, dull apathy, a painleſs pain,
  Yet will I come, and Thy deep Mercy prove:
For not in plaſtic feelings of the mind
Celeſtial comfort muſt I ſeek and find;
  But in true Preſence Thou art here, LORD
    CHRIST,
  Therefore I live for Thy dread Euchariſt.

Sorrowing yet rejoicing.

So many difappointments, woes, and cares,
   Fightings without, mifgiving fears within,
Heart-defolating joys, bewildering fnares,
   So great a daily load of unknown fin,
So wearily goes the world, fo heavily,
That it were better could I ceafe to be—
   Yea, but for Union unto Thee, LORD CHRIST;
   Therefore I live for Thy dread Eucharift.

Sacramental Reception.

A rufhing Sound as of a mighty Wind
   Came down from Heaven, and cloven Tongues
      of Flame
On every faithful brow their place did find:
   Not fo He cometh now; yet aye the Same,
With foft low breathings on the inmoft heart,
His unfeen fire of Love He doth impart,
   But chiefly at Thine Altar, O LORD CHRIST;
   Therefore I live for Thy dread Eucharift.

Awakening to Realities.

I gazed on phantom fhows and called them good,
   Dulling mine eyes with empty wearinefs;
I ate the hufks of fin, and thought it food,
   Till my poor cheated Soul fank down in dreari-
      nefs;
GOD's Grace awoke me; and I cried aloud—
Oh, fill my hungry Soul; fcatter this cloud;

There is no Light, nor Food, but Thou, Lord
    Christ;
Therefore I live for Thy dread Euchariſt.

Thirſt for Christ.

Not through mere ſhrinking from the griefs of hell,
   The worm that dies not, and the quenchleſs fire,
Not through mere longing evermore to dwell
   Among the radiant hoſts of Heaven's quire,
(For Heaven were hell if Thou Thy Face ſhouldſt
    hide,
And hell were Heaven if Thou ſhouldſt there
    abide :)
   Thyſelf, Thyſelf I long for, O Lord Christ;
Therefore I come to Thy dread Euchariſt.

Union with Christ.

Thou art aſcended : we may touch Thee now,
  By holy Faith which dwells in things above,
By holy Hope enduring things below,
  By Love, outſtripping both, repentant Love ;
Yea, and by this, combining all in one,
Faith, Hope, and Love in vaſt Communion,
   This more than Heavenly Teaching, O Lord
    Christ,
   This Gift of gifts, Thy glorious Euchariſt.

An Eucharistic Hymn of the xiii. Century.

Recolamus sacram Cænam.

CHRIST sits at His own Board;
    The Brethren twelve receive
    The Gift of Gladness; O my heart,
      Call up the solemn Eve.
He is our Maker, He
    Died on the Cross for us;
Oh, let us keep the memory
    Of His Last Supper thus:

He was about to leave
    The world, and pass away
Unto the FATHER; when He gave
    What He will give this day.
He ate the Paschal Lamb;
    He kept unto the last
The Law He issued; while He eat,
    That Law's stern letter passed.

Into His sacred Hands
    He took the Holy Bread;
He brake; He blessed each Fragment; then
    Unto His Brethren said—
Now take and eat ye This,
    This is My BODY given,
This is the Life laid down for you,
    This the New Law of Heaven.

And drink ye of this Cup;
 Oft as ye drink of Me,
I will ye do this I have done
 Unto My Memory.
He ſpake; before them all
 Still Perfect Man He ſtood,
Though what He ate and drank He named
 His Very Flesh and Blood.

He gave unto the Twelve
 (Not to His Manhood's loſs,
Not to Its outward change) the Gift,
 Fruit of the bitter Croſs.
And ever ſince that Day
 (Who may the Wonder tell?)
The Faithful eat of Christ, yet He
 Abides Unchangeable.

Whoever eats and drinks
 Aright, ſhall periſh never;
Whoever eats and drinks amiſs,
 Shall dwell in death for ever.
So let him cleanſe his Soul,
 Who wills what Jesus ſaith,
A bleſſed and an awful thing,
 Set unto Life or death.

O Living Bread, O Life,
 O Holy Jesus Christ,

Who art the fame in Heaven, though Thou
  On earth art facrificed;
Who in this lower world
  Doft feed the pure in heart,
Oh, grant us at the laft to be
  In Glory, where Thou art.

𝕿𝖍𝖊 𝕮𝖍𝖗𝖎𝖘𝖙𝖎𝖆𝖓 𝕬𝖑𝖙𝖆𝖗.

The Bread of GOD *is He Which cometh down from*
Heaven.

TREMBLING, we know that Thou, O
       LORD,
  Doft know us through all thought and
      word;
But fhed o'er all Thy BLOOD we fee,
So gladly hail our CHRIST in Thee.

Thus finding, as we have been found,
Thy feftive Table we furround;
In Thee contained, in Thee combined,
Bring Thee one offering and one mind.

Thou Bread of Life, upon Thy Tongue
When famifhed thoufands clofely hung,
Didft make the fainting body whole,
Come, ftrengthen and refrefh our Soul.

Thou, when the bridal wine ran dry,
A draught far richer didſt ſupply,
With real fulneſs of that hour,
Come cheer our Souls, Thy BLOOD outpour.

So bid us from Thy Board depart,
With all Thy Preſence in our heart,
And bear It far into the night
Of world and ſin, Thy Lamp of Light.

Chriſt All in All.

Omnia habemus in CHRISTO, *et omnia* CHRISTUS
eſt in nobis.

SAY, art thou wounded, feeble, weak?
In JESUS thy Phyſician ſeek;
Does fever ſtrike, or parching thirſt?
He is thy Fountain, beſt, and firſt;
Or, art thou bowed beneath ſin's load?
He is thy Juſtice—fly to GOD;
Does Soul or body ſickneſs thrall?
He is the Health of both, and all.

Liſt ye for help? Be not afraid,
He is thy near and ready Aid;
Does Death affright thee drawing near?
He is thy Life, and wherefore fear?

Long you for Heaven's eternal Day?
Walk boldly on, He is the Way;
He is thine Aid, His Life was given
To ope for thee the gates of Heaven.

If thou wouldſt fly the miſts of night,
The Sun of Juſtice is thy light;
He bids the tongue-tied Spirit ſpeak,
Unties it in Confeſſion meek:
Or ſeek ye Food? He gives thee Bread;
Thou art by Heavenly Manna fed:
O Hidden God, what harm can fall?
He gives Himſelf, He gives thee all.

Forgiveneſs in Communion.

Erlaſſen iſt der Sünden Schuld.

LOOSED are the bands thy Soul which
chained,
My FATHER's Love and Grace re-
gained—
Such are the words by which to-day
My SAVIOUR chaſed my grief away.

'Tis even ſo; His Death and Pain
God's Favour have reſtored again;
For me my higheſt Good is won,
The work of Grace is fully done.

Here Righteousneſs and Peace abound,
The feſtal robe I here have found,
Which covering all my guilt and ſin,
Has made my Soul at peace within.

This CHRIST hath wrought, my Bleſſed LORD,
Who feeds me at His gracious Board;
And gladneſs fills my heart and mind,
To think that pardon here I find.

Into my FATHER's Preſence dread,
No longer now I fear to tread;
His Wrath appeaſed through CHRIST, His SON,
He bids me come before His Throne.

He now regards me as His Child,
Since I through CHRIST am reconciled;
Waſhed in the BLOOD from JESU's Side,
To me Heaven's gate is opened wide.

Thy HOLY SPIRIT, CHRIST, impart,
Work true repentance in my heart,
And e'en from ſin's remoteſt brink
With deep abhorrence make me ſhrink;

That ſo I may not fall again,
By ſinning, into Satan's chain,
Nor throw my FATHER's Grace away,
By going any more aſtray.

So ſhall I die at peace with Thee,
From ſin and ſinner's doom ſet free,
And at the LAMB's own Marriage Feaſt,
In Heaven become a conſtant gueſt.

A Communion Hymn of the vii. Century.

Sancti, venite, CORPUS CHRISTI *ſumite.*

RAW nigh, and take the BODY of the
LORD,
And drink the Holy BLOOD for you
outpoured.

Saved by that BODY, hallowed by that BLOOD,
Whereby refreſhed, we render thanks to GOD.

Salvation's Giver, CHRIST the Only SON,
By that His Croſs and BLOOD the victory won.

Offered was He for greateſt and for leaſt,
Himſelf the Victim, and Himſelf the Prieſt.

Victims were offered by the Law of old,
That, in a type, celeſtial Myſteries told.

He, Ranſomer from death, and Light from ſhade,
Giveth His holy Grace His Saints to aid.

Approach ye then with faithful hearts ſincere,
And take the ſafeguard of Salvation here.

He that in this world rules His Saints, and ſhields,
To all believers Life Eternal yields ;

With Heavenly Bread makes them that hunger
　　　　whole,
Gives Living Waters to the thirſty Soul.

Alpha and Omega, to Whom ſhall bow
All nations at the Doom, is with us now.

The Soul's Soliloquy and Colloquy with Chriſt.

Schmücke dich olliebe Seele.

LEAVE, my Soul, the ſhades of darkneſs,
Deck thyſelf with robes of gladneſs,
With robes of pure and ſpotleſs white
Come to the ſource of Life and Light :
Even the loweſt and the leaſt
Are callèd to this Heavenly Feaſt ;
CHRIST of His Love and Mercy free
Will make His own Abode with thee.

Haſten to meet thy Loving LORD ;
He ſtandeth, knocking at the door.

Liften; His fweet and gentle Voice
Is calling thee; of His free Defire
He fpeaketh thus—Soul, whom I love,
My fpoufe, my undefiled, my dove,
Open to me; oh, let Me in,
Within thy heart, thy love to win.

Man will gladly, without meafure,
Spend much wealth, yea countlefs treafure,
To gain what his heart defireth:
Nor gold, nor filver GOD requireth—
Come to the Fountain, come and buy,
All ye who thirft; GOD from on high,
GOD gives Himfelf a Sacrifice:
Buy without money, without price.

It was, O Bleffed LORD, Thy Love,
Which made Thee leave Thy Throne above,
To fhed for us Thy Precious BLOOD,
That we, through that Life-giving Flood,
Cleanfèd might be from every ftain,
Might lift our eyes to Heaven again,
With GOD and FATHER reconciled
Through Thy great Love and Mercy mild.

I thirft, I faint, I long, I figh,
LORD JESU, draw in Mercy nigh;
My heart and ftrength have failed me,
For waiting, LORD, fo long for Thee.

Accept the homage that I bring,
My GOD, my SAVIOUR, and my King:
My LORD, my Light, my Life, my All,
Adoring at Thy Feet, I fall.

Oh, Myſtery of Myſteries,
Our GOD upon the Altar lies,
His FLESH our meat, His BLOOD our drink;
I long to come—and yet I ſhrink—
I'm all unworthy to draw near:
With trembling hope and loving fear,
I come, LORD, to Thy Heavenly Feaſt,
The laſt, the loweſt, and the leaſt
Of all Thy gueſts; imploring Thee,
My Soul from ſin and ſtain ſet free,
Send Thy Sweet SPIRIT to my heart,
That I may ſee Thee as Thou art,
To make me pure, a fit abode
For Thee, my SAVIOUR and my GOD.

LORD JESUS, of Thy wondrous Love,
Make me Thy gueſt in Heaven above
When I have drunk my cup of woe,
And learnt to bear Thy Croſs below,
And through the ſhades of death have paſſed:
LORD JESU, grant me at the laſt
To be Thy thankful, happy gueſt
At the LAMB's glorious Marriage Feaſt.

The Tree of Life.

Signum pretiofius, Signum Crucis pretiofius.

HAIL! faving Crofs, hail! facred Sign,
  More precious this than gold approved
    By threefold fire, or brighteft gem:
  Here, at thy foot, I would recline,
Moft fure by this, how GOD has loved
  The Catholic Jerufalem.

Here would I lay my weary thought,
  Too weary long, too long oppreft
    Beneath the weight of finful load:
  Here would I feek repofe, long fought,
  But fought in vain, in the unreft
    And tumult of deftruction's road.

Here, 'neath the Shelter-Tree of Life,
  Is refuge from the pelting blaft,
    And fhadow from the heat of day:
  Here, from the burthen, jar, and ftrife
  Of empty trifles, paffing, paft,
    Here would I reft alway.

The troubled heart finds here repofe,
  And here the angry paffions lull;
    The fenfual appetite is checked,
  And here increafe of Love ftill grows
  More pure, till its fruition full
    Unclouds the opening intellect.

Hail! ſaving Croſs, hail! ſaving Sign,
 What gems of earth may countervail
  That ſource of Love, that ſpring of Faith:
Oh, wondrous depth of Love Divine,
 Once and again the Croſs I hail,
  Our only hope in life and death.

The Euchariſtic Advent.

I came down from Heaven, not to do Mine own Will,
but the Will of Him that ſent Me.

E cometh—on yon hallowed Board
 The ready Feaſt doth duly ſhow,
Where wait the Chalice and the Bread,
 Like gems within their veil of ſnow.

He cometh—as He came of old,
 Suddenly to His Father's Shrine,
Into the hearts He died to make
 Meet temples for His Grace Divine.

He cometh—as the Bridegroom comes
 Unto the Feaſt Himſelf has ſpread;
His FLESH and BLOOD the Heavenly Food
 Wherewith the wedding gueſts are fed.

He cometh—gentle as the dew,
 And ſweet as drops of honey clear,
And good as GOD's Own Manna-ſhower,
 To longing Souls that meet Him here.

He cometh—let not one withdraw,
  Nor fear to bring repented ſin;
There's BLOOD to waſh, there's BREAD to feed,
  And CHRIST Himſelf to enter in.

He cometh—praiſes in the Church
  And hymns of praiſe in Heaven above,
And in our hearts repentant faith,
  And love that ſprings to meet His Love.

Commemoration of a Faithful Prieſt.

Quantis micas honoribus.

OOD Prieſt, where art thou hid from
          human eyes
        In calm Repoſe,
      Haply to tread the marble-ſhining ſkies
  After life's woes;
Where GOD's Own Preſence hath His People bleſt,
Himſelf their happy Guerdon, and their Reſt.

Thoſe Virtues, in whoſe ſteps thou here didſt toil,
      And ſtrive to go,
Are not put off with this thy fleſhly coil,
      And left below;
They now are turned to rays of Light Divine,
And glorious Crowns, which on thy temples
          ſhine.

And they for whom thou toiledſt in ſecond birth,
    With many a ſigh,
Are with thee, like thy children, fled from earth,
    And through the ſky
They ſhare thy victory the bleſt Choirs among,
And lift with thee the new myſterious Song.

Thou here below, dim-veiled from earthly eyes
    In ſhadows dread,
Didſt offer up th' Unbloody Sacrifice,
    On CHRIST to feed;
He now Himſelf, with Unveiled DEITY,
Of Spirits Immortal the Repaſt ſhall be.

And as a daily Sacrifice may we
    Be lifted up,
Bearing our daily Croſs, and ſhare with thee
    Thy Maſter's Cup:
We preſs, like ſhipwrecked ſailors on the wave,
To Shores where CHRIST doth ſtretch His Arms
    to ſave.

To Him, Who governs His own Prieſtly Hoſt,
    Himſelf their Crown;
To Him with FATHER and with HOLY GHOST,
    Be all renown:
All praiſe to Him as hath been heretofore,
All praiſe to Him both now and evermore.

The True Vine.

I am the True Vine.

WHEN Ifrael lay in Kadefh, where Paran's wilds expand,
Into the north twelve mighty men were fent to fpy the Land;
Each Tribe gave in its kinglieft before the hofts of light
Rofe up all in JEHOVAH'S Name to fpoil the Amorite.

Down in the fertile valley, where Efhcol's waters roll,
They felled the lordly Cedar-tree and wrought it to a pole,
And then they turned them fouth again and bare to Ifrael's line
The firft-fruits of the Gift of GOD, the firft-ripe of the Vine.

And what to us (the world exclaims) that Vine-branch borne of two?
O fools and blinded—is it not a figure of the True?
It is the fum of all things; yea, that deed of pre-fcience done
Speaks of two Difpenfations, and the Gift that made them one.

They who were Grace-expectant, they who lived
      and died in Grace;
They who ſaw Christ far off, and they who ſee,
      though veiled, His Face:
Thoſe went before; theſe follow: they are all
      one Brotherhood,
And in the midſt the True Vine hangs upon the
      holy Rood.

O Tree of Life, O Vine of God, Thou art amid
      us now;
The Bread we break, the Wine we bleſs, are they
      not very Thou?
Veiled in His Creatures comes our God; He
      comes Who dwells above,
The altogether Lovely, and the Fount and Life
      of Love.

Oh, come, ye heavy-laden, and henceforth reſtful
      be;
Oh, come, your weary weight of ſin long ſince was
      laid on Me—
This is Thy Call, O Merciful; to all who will is
      given
To eat Supernal Bread and drink the Myſtic Wine
      of Heaven.

Ah, in our boſom's Hebron the Son of Anak
      dwells
'Mid pride-built walls, embattled towers, and
      Heav'n-high citadels;

More faithlefs than the faithlefs ten, we will not
    break that fway;
We think to win the pleafant Land, but not the
    Crofs's way.

Oh, firft with Grace preparing, then with Gift no
    tongue can fhow,
Lion of Judah, vifit us ; true Jofhua, fmite our foe ;
Come from Thy Altar to our hearts, our Health,
    our Food to be ;
And caft imaginations down, and fubject all to
    Thee.

Then not alone our fathers, Thy Prefence fhall
    bring nigh :
Angels, Archangels, fing with us, and all Heav'n's
    Company ;
And now, what reck we ills to come ? They can-
    not mar our reft ;
Our Love is ours and we are His ; we want not;
    we are bleft.

Ebe moft Precious Blood of Chrift.

Salvete! Christi *Vulnera.*

HAIL ! holy Wounds of Jesus, hail !
    Sweet Pledges of the faving Rood,
    Whence flow the Streams that never
        fail,
The purple Streams of His Dear Blood.

Brighter than brighteſt ſtars ye ſhow,
    Than ſweeteſt roſe your ſcent more rare,
No Indian gem may match your glow,
    No honey's taſte with yours compare.

Portals ye are to that dear home
    Wherein our wearied Souls may hide,
Whereto no angry foe can come,
    The Heart of JESUS crucified.

What countleſs ſtripes our JESUS bore,
    All naked left in Pilate's hall;
What copious Floods of purple Gore
    Through rents in His torn Garments fall.

His beauteous Brow, oh, ſhame and grief,
    By the ſharp thorny Crown is riven;
Through Hands and Feet, without relief,
    The cruel nails are rudely driven.

But, when for our poor ſakes He died,
    A willing Prieſt by Love ſubdued,
The ſoldier's lance transfixed His Side,
    Forth flowed the Water and the BLOOD.

That bitter Torment He endured,
    Full Ranſom for our Souls to give,
Till from His racking Frame was poured
    Each Drop of BLOOD, that we might live.

Come, bathe you in that healing Flood,
   All ye who mourn, by guilt oppreſt,
Your only hope is Jesu's Blood,
   His ſacred Heart your only reſt.

All praiſe to Him, the Eternal Son,
   At God's Right Hand enthroned above,
Whoſe Blood our full Redemption won,
   Whoſe Spirit ſeals the Gift of Love.

A Communion Hymn from Calderon.

Which things are an Allegory.

HONEY in the lion's mouth,
    Emblem myſtical, Divine,
    How the ſweet and ſtrong combine ;
   Cloven Rock for Iſrael's drouth ;
  Treaſure-houſe of golden grain,
By our Joſeph laid in ſtore,
In His brethren's famine ſore
   Freely to diſpenſe again ;
Dew on Gideon's ſnowy fleece ;
  Well from bitter changed to ſweet ;
  Shewbread laid in order meet ;
Bread whoſe coſt doth ne'er increaſe,
  Though no rain in April fall ;
Horeb's Manna, freely given,
Showered in white dew from Heaven,
  Marvellous, Angelical ;

Weightieſt Bunch of Canaan's Vine;
Cake to ſtrengthen and ſuſtain
Through long days of deſert pain;
Salem's monarch's Bread and Wine:—
Thou the Antidote ſhall be
Of my ſickneſs and my ſin,
Conſolation, Medicine,
Life and Sacrament to me.

PART III.

THE CONSECRATION.

Sequence of S. Thomas Aquinas.

Lauda, Sion, Salvatorem.

LAUD, O Sion, thy Salvation,
    Laud, with hymns of exultation,
        Christ, thy King and Shepherd
            true ;
    Bring Him all the praiſe thou
        knoweſt ;
He is more than thou beſtoweſt ;
    Never canſt thou reach His due.

Special theme for glad thankſgiving
Is the Living and Life-giving
    Bread, to-day before thee ſet ;
From His Hands of old partaken
As we know by faith unſhaken,
    Where the Twelve at ſupper met.

Full and clear ring out thy chanting,
Joy nor sweetest grace be wanting,
  From thy heart let praises burst;
For to-day the Feast is holden
When the Institution olden
  Of that Supper is rehearsed.

Here the new Law's new Oblation
By the new King's Revelation
  Ends the form of ancient Rite;
Now the New the old effaces,
Truth away the shadow chases,
  Light dispels the gloom of night.

What He did, at supper seated,
Christ ordained to be repeated,
  His Memorial ne'er to cease;
And His Rule for guidance taking,
Bread and Wine we hallow, making
  Thus our Sacrifice of Peace.

Wondrous truth by Christians learnèd,
Bread into His Flesh is turnèd,
  Into Precious Blood the Wine;
Sight hath failed, nor thought conceiveth,
But a dauntless faith believeth,
  Resting on a Power Divine.

Whoso of this Food partaketh
Rendeth not the Lord, nor breaketh;
  Christ is Whole to all that taste;

Thousands are, as one, receivers;
One, as thousands of believers,
   Eats of Him Who cannot waste.

Bad and good the Feast are sharing;
Oh, what diverse dooms preparing,
   Endless death, or endless Life:
Life to these, to those damnation:
See how like participation
   Is with unlike issues rife.

When the Sacrament is broken,
Doubt not, but believe 'tis spoken,
That each severed outward Token
   Doth the very Whole contain:
Nought the precious Gift divideth,
Breaking but the Sign betideth,
JESUS still the same abideth,
   Still Unbroken doth remain.

Lo, the Angels' FOOD is given
To the pilgrim who hath striven;
See the children's Bread from Heaven
   Which on dogs may not be spent:
Truth the ancient Types fulfilling,
Isaac bound, a Victim willing;
Paschal Lamb, its Life-blood spilling;
   Manna, to the Fathers sent.

Very Bread, Good Shepherd, tend us,
JESU, of Thy Love befriend us;

Thou refrefh us, Thou defend us,
Thine eternal Goodnefs fend us
    In the land of Life to fee :
Thou, Who all things canft and knoweft,
Who on earth fuch Food beftoweft,
Grant us with Thy Saints, though loweft,
Where the Heavenly Feaft Thou fhoweft,
    Fellow heirs and guefts to be.

Corpus Chrifti.

*O come, let us worfhip, and fall down, and kneel before
the* LORD *our Maker.*

JESUS, my LORD, my GOD, my All,
    How can I love Thee as I ought,
    And how revere this wondrous Gift,
    So far furpaffing hope or thought ?
Sweet Sacrament, we Thee adore ;
Oh, make us love Thee more and more.

Had I but Mary's finlefs heart
    To love Thee with, my deareft King,
Oh, with what burfts of fervent praife
    Thy Goodnefs, JESUS, would I fing.
    Sweet Sacrament, we Thee adore ;
    Oh, make us love Thee more and more.

Ah, fee, within a creature's hand
    The vaft Creator deigns to be,

Repoſing infant-like, as though
  On Joſeph's arm, or Mary's knee.
    Sweet Sacrament, we Thee adore;
    Oh, make us love Thee more and more.

Thy BODY, SOUL, and GODHEAD, all,
  O Myſtery of Love Divine,
I cannot compaſs all I have,
  For all Thou haſt and art are mine.
    Sweet Sacrament, we Thee adore;
    Oh, make us love Thee more and more.

Sound, ſound His praiſes higher ſtill,
  And come, ye Angels, to our aid,
'Tis GOD, 'tis GOD, the Very GOD,
  Whoſe Power both men and Angels made.
    Sweet Sacrament, we Thee adore;
    Oh, make us love Thee more and more.

Ring joyouſly, ye ſolemn bells,
  And wave, oh, wave, ye cenſers bright,
'Tis JESUS cometh, Mary's SON,
  And GOD of GOD, and Light of Light.
    Sweet Sacrament, we Thee adore;
    Oh, make us love Thee more and more.

O earth, grow flowers beneath His Feet,
  And thou, O ſun, ſhine bright this day,
He comes, He comes, oh, Heaven on earth,
  Our JESUS comes upon His Way.
    Sweet Sacrament, we Thee adore;
    Oh, make us love Thee more and more.

He comes, He comes, the LORD of Hofts,
    Borne on His Throne triumphantly;
We fee Thee, and we know Thee, LORD,
    And yearn to fhed our blood for Thee.
      Sweet Sacrament, we Thee adore;
      Oh, make us love Thee more and more.

Our hearts leap up; our trembling fong
    Grows fainter ftill; we can no more:
Silence, and let us weep—and die
    Of very love, while we adore.
      Great Sacrament of Love Divine,
      All, all we have or are be Thine.

Anima Chrifti.

Anima CHRISTI, *fanctifica me.*

SOUL of JESU, make me holy,
    Make me contrite, meek, and lowly;
    SOUL moft Stainlefs, SOUL Divine,
    Cleanfe this fordid Soul of mine;
Hallow this polluted Soul,
Purify it, make it whole;
SOUL of JESUS, hallow me;
         Miferere DOMINE.

Save me, BODY of my LORD,
Save a finner vile, abhorred;

Sacred Body, wan and worn,
Bruiſed and mangled, ſcourged and torn,
Pierced Hands, and Feet, and Side,
Rent, inſulted, crucified,
Save me—to the Croſs I flee;
          Miſerere Domine.

Blood of Jesus, Stream of Life,
Sacred Stream with Bleſſings rife,
From that Broken Body ſhed
On the Croſs that Altar dread;
Given to be our Drink Divine,
Fill my heart, and make it Thine;
Blood of Christ, my ſuccour be;
          Miſerere Domine.

Holy Water, Stream that poured
From Thy riven Side, O Lord,
Waſh Thou me without, within;
Cleanſe me from the taint of ſin,
Till my Soul is clean and white,
Bathed, and purified, and bright,
As a ranſomed Soul ſhould be;
          Miſerere Domine.

Jesu, by the wondrous Power
Of Thine awful Paſſion hour,
By the unimagined Woe
Mortal man may never know;
By the Curſe upon Thee laid,

By the Ranſom Thou haſt paid,
By Thy Paſſion comfort me ;
                  Miſerere DOMINE.

JESU, by Thy bitter Death,
By Thy laſt expiring Breath,
Give me the eternal Life
Purchaſed by that mortal Strife ;
Thou didſt ſuffer Death, that I
Might not die eternally ;
By Thy Dying quicken me ;
                  Miſerere DOMINE.

Miſerere ; let me be
Never parted, LORD, from Thee ;
Guard me from my ruthleſs foe,
Save me from eternal Woe ;
In the dreadful Judgment Day
Be Thy Croſs my hope and ſtay ;
When the hour of death is near,
And my Spirit faints for fear,
Call me with Thy Voice of Love,
Place me near to Thee above,
With Thine Angel Hoſt to raiſe
An undying ſong of praiſe ;
                  Miſerere DOMINE.

An Ancient Act of Adoration.

Ave! Christi Corpus *Verum.*

AIL ! O Flesh of Christ Divine,
Hail ! O ſweet and ruddy Wine,
Blood the Cup and Flesh the Meat,
And in each is Christ complete.

This is He, the Bridegroom, dight
In His Veſture red and white ;
White, for Him a Virgin bore,
Red, for He His Blood did pour.

By the Wounds, and ſtripes, and ſcorn,
By the Paſſion Thou haſt borne,
Hear us, Jesu, when we call,
From deſtruction ſave us all.

A Sequence of the xvi. Century.

Laureata Plebs fidelis.

OW let the Faithful come, with joy re-
vering
The Sacramental Christ this day,
Rendering the moſt high King meet
praiſe, and wearing,
Through Him, the conqueror's bay.

What if the place whence He rules all be Heaven?
　Oh, He deigns elſewhere to abide,
And day by day to loving hearts is given,
　He, Who was crucified.

Behold the Price, which bought the holy Nation,
　The Grace which ſpeaks of Grace to come,
And all the Virtue of His ſacred Paſſion
　Have here this earthly Germ:
All Gifts are here to give the which He ſuffered,
　All Gifts with which the DOVE came down;
Therefore aright the Sacrifice be offered,
　Of all the Fruit and Crown.

This did men ſee far off, and died confeſſing,
　This did Melchizedek declare,
Offering the Bread of Life and Wine of Bleſſing
　To GOD, before they were;
And erſt they ſlew a Lamb, the time foreſhowing
　When that Lamb's ſlaughter ſhould give place
(The BLOOD of CHRIST, world-cleanſing Stream,
　　faſt flowing)
　Unto the True LAMB's Grace.

One link yet more 'twixt men whom ages ſever,
　'Tis Manna, Bread ſent down to tell
The WORD made FLESH ſhould be made Food
　　for ever
　To the true Iſrael:

That Bread was food of time, This is Eternal :
  That came the flefh alone to feed,
But This is Life and Health and Joy fupernal ;
  This Cup is Drink indeed.

Lo, without price abundant Peace is given,
  The poor and needy here may come ;
O happy Feaft for citizens of Heaven,
  Lead, through the ftrange land, home ;
O Path of Life, Refrefhment never cloying,
  O Christ, Perennial Light, give Life ;
Lo, our part be with Souls the Blifs enjoying
  In Thy clear Vifion rife.

Give us Thyfelf. Thou art the Wave Immortal,
  The Fruitful Vine, the Living Bread ;
So at the laft we mifs not Sion's portal,
  We would be cleanfed and fed :
It is Thy Death which in thefe Gifts is fpeaking,
  Oh, may we lift to It alone,
And we fhall find the Country we are feeking,
  We fhall be nigh Thy Throne.

𝕾acramental 𝕳ymn.

He that eateth Me, the fame fhall live by Me.

GOD, Unfeen, yet ever near,
  Thy Prefence may we feel ;
And, thus infpired with holy fear,
  Before Thine Altar kneel.

Here may Thy faithful People know
    The Bleſſings of Thy Love,
The Streams that through the deſert flow,
    The Manna from above.

We come, obedient to Thy Word,
    To feaſt on Heavenly Food;
Our Meat, the Body of the Lord,
    Our Drink, His Precious Blood.

Thus may we all Thy Words obey,
    For we, O God, are Thine;
And go rejoicing on our way,
    Renewed with Strength Divine.

A Hymn attributed to S. Anſelm.

Christi Corpus, *Ave!*

HAIL! Flesh of Christ, of Holy Virgin
    born;
    Hail! Undivided Deity,
The Way, the Life, the Health of man
    forlorn,
Set us from all ill free.

Hail! Blood of Christ, moſt holy Drink of
    Heaven,
    Mighty to waſh away all ſtain;
Hail! Blood, Which flowed forth when the Side
    was riven
    Upon the Croſs of pain.

An Ancient Eucharistic Prayer.

My Flesh *is Meat indeed, and My* Blood *is Drink indeed.*

O LIVING Bread from Heaven,
To weary pilgrims given,
   Angelic ſuſtenance ;
Celeſtial Food, I need Thee,
Thou, Thou alone canſt feed me ;
   My Life comes only thence.

O Fount of Love abounding,
My wondering thoughts confounding,
   I come to taſte Thy ſtream ;
From His warm Heart that's bleeding,
To give me what is needing
   To quicken, cheer, redeem.

O Jesu, here Thou'rt hidden,
Here now, as I am bidden,
   By faith I feaſt on Thee ;
Oh, let the clouds concealing,
Soon melt away, revealing
   The God I long to ſee.

To God our Great Creator,
To God, Who took our nature,
   To God the Holy Dove,

The THREE in ONE, be given
Eternal praiſe in Heaven
And earth, in ſongs of Love.

Chriſt our High Prieſt and Sacrifice.

Mundus effuſis Redemptus.

SING, O earth, for thy redemption,
 Lo, His race of torment run,
CHRIST the Sanctuary enters,
 Prieſt and Victim both in One ;
There to make our peace with GOD,
By th' Oblation of His BLOOD.

Guilty, for the guilty pleading,
 Legal Prieſt, thy taſk is o'er ;
Goats and oxen—empty ſhadows—
 There is need of you no more ;
 Not ſuch feeble things as theſe
 Could an Angry GOD appeaſe.

Hail to Thee, High Prieſt eternal ;
 Prieſt without a ſpot of ſin ;
Veiled of old in myſtic figures,
 Holy, Infinite, Divine ;
 Thou art He Whoſe BLOOD alone
 Can for human guilt atone.

Thou, of Life the LORD Anointed,
  Led to Thy self-chosen doom,
That same Flesh which Thou hast moulded
  In Thy Virgin Mother's Womb,
    Offerest on the Holy Rood,
    Man for man, and GOD to GOD.

While the rage of Thy tormentors
  In its very fury blind,
As from Thy pure Veins it madly
  Pours the Ransom of mankind,
    Does but work Thy own Decree,
    Fixed from all Eternity.

The Unsearchable Riches of Christ in the Blessed Sacrament.

The LORD *is my stony Rock, and my Defence, my* SAVIOUR, *my* GOD, *and my Might in Whom I will trust, my Buckler, the Horn also of my Salvation, and my Refuge.*

SWEET Sacrament Divine,
    Hid in Thine earthly Home,
  Lo, round Thy lowly Shrine,
    With suppliant hearts we come;
  JESUS, to Thee our voice we raise,
    In Songs of love and heartfelt praise,
  Sweet Sacrament Divine.

Sweet Sacrament of Peace,
  Dear Home for every heart,

Where reſtleſs yearnings ceaſe,
  And ſorrows all depart ;
There in Thine Ear, all truſtfully,
We tell our tale of miſery,
Sweet Sacrament of Peace.

Sweet Sacrament of Reſt,
  Ark from the ocean's roar,
Within Thy Shelter bleſt,
  Soon may we reach the ſhore ;
  Save us, for ſtill the tempeſt raves,
  Save, leſt we ſink beneath the waves,
Sweet Sacrament of Reſt.

Sweet Sacrament Divine,
  Earth's Light and Jubilee,
In Thy far depths doth ſhine
  Thy GODHEAD's Majeſty ;
  Sweet Light, ſo ſhine on us, we pray,
  That earthly joys may fade away,
Sweet Sacrament Divine.

Proceſſional Hymn of S. Thomas Aquinas, for Maundy Thurſday.

Pange Lingua Glorioſi CORPORIS.

NOW my tongue the Myſtery telling,
  Of the Glorious Body ſing,
And the BLOOD, all price excelling,
  Which the Gentiles' LORD and
     KING,

In a Virgin's Womb once dwelling,
  Shed for this world's ranſoming.

Given for us, and condeſcending
  To be born for us below,
He with men in converſe blending
  Dwelt, the ſeed of Truth to ſow,
Till He cloſed with wondrous ending
  His moſt patient Life of woe.

That laſt night, at Supper lying,
  'Mid the Twelve, His choſen band,
JESUS, with the Law complying,
  Keeps the feaſt its rites demand ;
Then, more Precious Food ſupplying,
  Gives Himſelf with His own Hand.

WORD-MADE-FLESH true Bread He maketh
  By His Word His FLESH to be ;
Wine, His BLOOD, Which whoſo taketh
  Muſt from carnal thoughts be free ;
Faith alone, though ſight forſaketh,
  Shows true hearts the Myſtery.

Therefore we, before Him bending,
  This great Sacrament revere ;
Types and ſhadows have their ending,
  For the newer Rite is here ;
Faith, our outward ſenſe befriending,
  Makes our inward viſion clear.

Glory let us give, and Blessing
  To the FATHER and the SON,
Honour, Might, and Praise addressing,
  While eternal ages run;
Ever too, His Love confessing,
  Who from BOTH with BOTH is ONE.

An Eucharistic Hymn of the xv. Century.

Ave! Rex, Qui descendisti.

HAIL! O King, Who hither wendedst
  From the skies, and condescendedst
    In a fleshly form to dwell:
Hail! O BODY True and Holy,
Of a Virgin pure and lowly
    Born, to crush the might of Hell.

Hail! O WORD, Incarnate truly,
Virgin-born, before Whom duly
    We in faith undoubting fall:
Hail to Thee! Who, scourged in malice,
Drankest of the bitter Chalice,
    Mingled vinegar and gall.

Hail to Thee! Who didst not falter
On the Cross's mournful Altar,
    Dying there in sharpest pain:

Hail to Thee! Whoſe one Oblation
Saved the world from condemnation,
   Burſt the gates of Hell in twain.

Hail! Thou Brightneſs ever glorious,
Hail! Thou FLESH of CHRIST victorious,
   Flower and Fruit of Virgin Womb,
Hail! Thou Bread by Angels ſharèd,
Hail! Thou Light for Saints preparèd,
   Saviour of the World from doom.

Hail! Thou meek Redeemer, ſending
Mercies to us never-ending,
   Thou who ſootheſt hapleſs men:
Hail! O CHRIST, the FATHER's Splendour,
Grant, I pray, Thy Mercy tender,
   Now and evermore.

A Prayer after Conſecration, of the xii. Century.

Salve! Sancta CARO DEI.

SACRED FLESH of GOD, by Whom
   Guilty men are ſaved from doom,
   Setting us Thy ſervants free,
   When Thou hangedſt on the tree.

   Piercèd BODY, iſſuing thence,
   Water cleanſed from that offence
   Done by diſobedient man,
   When creation firſt began.

Wash me in the healing Flood,
Sacred BODY, of Thy BLOOD;
Cleanse Thou me from every stain,
Rescue me from endless pain.

Me of Thy great Goodness bless
With eternal Happiness;
By Thy Sanctity made whole,
Strengthen and sustain my Soul.

Make mine enemies to fall,
Into friends convert them all;
King of Angels, crush their pride,
And their hatred turn aside.

Thou, Who art of Life the Door,
With Thy BODY me restore;
Thou in death's extremest hour
Save me by Thy mighty Power,

From the roaring lion's wrath,
From the strength the dragon hath;
Give, with Faith and Hope unfailing,
Charity o'er all prevailing.

𝕬 𝕷𝖎𝖙𝖆𝖓𝖞 𝖔𝖋 𝕵𝖊𝖘𝖚𝖘, 𝕻𝖗𝖊𝖘𝖊𝖓𝖙 𝖎𝖓 𝖙𝖍𝖊 𝕭𝖑𝖊𝖘𝖘𝖊𝖉 𝕾𝖆𝖈𝖗𝖆𝖒𝖊𝖓𝖙.

I am Thy Servant.

LORD, my King and Master Thou,
To Whom the choirs of Angels bow,
Before Thine Altar prostrate now;
My JESU, look on me.

Thou, with Thine own moſt Precious BLOOD,
Haſt bought me for Thyſelf, my GOD;
Thine eaſy Yoke, is all my load;
   My JESU, give it me.

I love it, LORD; it is my choice
To follow Thee, and know Thy Voice;
In this bleſt ſlavery, I rejoice;
   My JESU, bind Thou me.

Bind me eternally to Thee,
With bonds, which only bind to free,
Let cords of Love my fetters be;
   My JESU, draw Thou me.

Thine am I, LORD, for ever Thine;
I to Thy Majeſty Divine
All that I am, or have, reſign;
   My JESU, reign in me.

Lo, at Thy Feet, I wait Thy Will,
Let that alone my being fill,
All earthly paſſions calm and ſtill;
   My JESU, work in me.

Each thought to Thee, my Sovereign dear,
Subdue; let nought of earth draw near;
In ſilence I Thy Voice would hear;
   My JESU, ſpeak in me.

Here, in Thy Bleſſed Sacrament,
With eye, and ear, and heart attent,
I wait Thy Grace's bleſt deſcent;
   My JESU, viſit me.

My Lord and Master, can it be
That Thou shouldst gird Thyself, on me
To wait, in Thy Humility;
          My Jesu, humble me.

Nay, more, Thyself the Very Bread
Wherewith Thine ingrate slave is fed,
Oh, who can such a service dread?
          My Jesu, feed Thou me.

Adorable and gracious King,
My heart is all I have to bring,
Spurn not th' unworthy offering;
          My Jesu, own Thou me.

Oh, make it cleave to Thee alway,
So in Thine awful Reckoning Day,
Thou to this humbling Soul mayst say—
          My Jesu, grant it me.

Well done, My Servant, good and true;
Enter the Joy prepared for you,
Joy, that earth's thraldom never knew—
          My Jesu, claim Thou me.

My Lord, one boon I ask of Thee—
Oh, let this feeble service be
Perfected in Eternity;
          My Jesu, ever rule Thou me.

The Rhyme of S. Thomas Aquinas.

Adoro Te devote, Latens Deitas.

GODHEAD Hid, devoutly I adore
    Thee,
Who truly art within the Forms before
    me;
To Thee my heart I bow with bended knee,
As failing quite in contemplating Thee.
    Jesu, eternal Shepherd, hear our cry;
    Increaſe the faith of all whoſe Souls on Thee rely.

Sight, touch, and taſte in Thee are each deceived;
The ear alone moſt ſafely is believed;
I believe all the Son of God hath ſpoken,
Than Truth's own Word there is no ſurer token.
    Jesu, eternal Shepherd, hear our cry;
    Increaſe the faith of all whoſe Souls on Thee rely.

God only on the Croſs lay hid from view;
But here, lies hid at once the Manhood too;
And I, in both profeſſing my belief,
Make the ſame prayer as the repentant thief.
    Jesu, eternal Shepherd, hear our cry;
    Increaſe the faith of all whoſe Souls on Thee rely.

Thy Wounds, as Thomas ſaw, I do not ſee;
Yet Thee confeſs, my Lord and God to be:

Make me believe Thee ever more and more;
In Thee my hope, in Thee my love to ſtore.
   Jesu, eternal Shepherd, hear our cry,
   Increaſe the faith of all whoſe Souls on Thee rely.

O Thou Memorial of our Lord's own Dying,
O Living Bread, to mortals Life ſupplying,
Make Thou my Soul henceforth on Thee to live;
Ever a taſte of Heavenly ſweetneſs give.
   Jesu, eternal Shepherd, hear our cry;
   Increaſe the faith of all whoſe Souls on Thee rely.

O loving Pelican, O Jesu, Lord,
Unclean I am, but cleanſe me in Thy Blood;
Of Which a ſingle Drop, for ſinners ſpilt,
Can purge the entire world from all its guilt.
   Jesu, eternal Shepherd, hear our cry;
   Increaſe the faith of all whoſe Souls on Thee rely.

Jesu, Whom for the preſent Veiled I ſee,
What I ſo thirſt for, oh, vouchſafe to me;
That I may ſee Thy Countenance unfolding,
And may be bleſt Thy Glory in beholding.
   Jesu, eternal Shepherd, hear our cry;
   Increaſe the faith of all whoſe Souls on Thee rely.

An Ancient Act of Adoration.

Ave! Caro Christi *Cara.*

HAIL! Flesh of Christ, Beloved Ob-
    lation,
   Sacrifice for our Salvation,
    On the Crofs a Victim flain :
Oh, by that, Thy Death of fadnefs,
Raife us decked in light and gladnefs,
   With Thee glorified to reign.

Hail! Word Incarnate, Which Divineft,
Hallowed on the Altar fhineft ;
   Bread of Angels Ever-living,
   Health and Hope to mortals giving,
   Antidote, all guilt relieving.
Hail! Thou Body of Christ Jesus,
Heaven-defcended to releafe us,
Thy redeemed from ruin buying,
On the Crofs when nailed and dying.

The Pledge of Immortality.

My Flesh *is Meat indeed, and My* Blood *is
Drink indeed.*

BREAD of the World, in Mercy broken,
   Wine of the World, in Mercy fhed,
   By Whom the Words of Life were
    fpoken,
And in Whofe Death our fins are dead ;

Look on the heart, by ſorrow broken,
Look on the tears, by ſinners ſhed,
And be Thy Feaſt to us the Token
That by Thy Grace our Souls are fed.

A Prayer, after Confecration, of the xb. Century.

Ave! Verbum Incarnatum.

HAIL! Holy FLESH of JESUS CHRIST,
    Upon the Altar lying,
Laſt Gift of the Incarnate WORD
    Before His precious Dying.
Hail! Living BREAD of Angels bright,
    Who wrought'ſt Redemption's ſtory,
Thou Hope of each one named from Thee,
    We give Thee thanks and glory.

Euchariſtic Meditation.

This is My BODY. *This is My* BLOOD.

HOLY JESUS, we believe
    That Thou art Preſent here,
With heart and Soul we ſurely know
    Our Deareſt LORD is near ;
For, though Thy Bleſſed Preſence
Is not viſibly revealed,

Faith tells us, in thefe Sacred Forms,
  Thou art indeed concealed:
On bended knee then let us pray
  That Thou mayft be adored
For aye, in Thy Dread Eucharift,
  O Thou moft Gracious LORD.

How great fhould be our reverence,
  How great the love and fear,
With which, to this High Sacrament
  In faith we fhould draw near;
Our hearts fhould be all purified,
  From earthly care fet free,
Feeling their own unworthinefs,
  And full of love for Thee;
O Thou, our own Beloved LORD,
  Our SAVIOUR, and our Friend,
Look down with Thine All-pitying Eye,
  On us Thy Bleffing fend.

We know our fins are manifold,
  Yet ftill to Thee we fly,
Trufting that in Thy Mercy great
  Thou wilt receive our cry;
For where elfe can we hope to find
  Forgivenefs full and free,
Except in Thine own Sacraments,
  When, LORD, we come to Thee?
Then, JESU, Prieft and Shepherd True,
  Grant Pardon, when we ftray

Without Thy Flock, of which Thou art
   The Life, the Truth, the Way.

And when our hearts bowed down with woe,
   Nor reſt nor comfort find,
We come to Thee, O Saviour Dear,
   Of Comforters moſt kind ;
For, when Thou giveſt us Thyſelf,
   O Precious Bread of Life,
In wondering awe we muſe not on
   Our Soul's moſt bitter ſtrife,
Feeling that Thou doſt then abide
   In us, Thou Prince of Peace ;
And that Thy Bleſſed Preſence, Lord,
   Hath cauſed our grief to ceaſe.

So too, when ſome bright beam of joy,
   E'en though of earth it be,
Lights up our ſtar of hope, then, Lord,
   We gladly fly to Thee,
Knowing that Thou, moſt Pitiful,
   Haſt ſent this gladſome ray
To ſhed a brightneſs o'er our path
   Which cheers our onward way ;
Lord Jesu, bleſs our earthly joys,
   Thou, Who our woes haſt healed,
And be Thou, in our hopes and fears,
   Our Helper and our Shield.

When death is drawing near, and when
   In dread our Spirits fail,

Lord Jesu, ſtill abide with us
  Through the dark gloomy Vale;
In Thy moſt Bleſſed Euchariſt,
  Give us Thyſelf once more,
That in the Strength of that Sweet Food,
  Our life's ſad journey o'er,
We may the Heavenly City reach,
  Where, freed from all alarms,
Our Souls ſhall find eternal Reſt
  In Thy Almighty Arms.

An Act of Adoration to the Body of Christ, of the xiv. Century.

Ave! Caro Christi *Cara.*

HAIL! Flesh of Christ; hail! Sweet-
    eſt Food,
  Upon the Altar of the Rood
    A Sacred Victim laid;
By that Thy Paſſion grant us Grace
To dwell with Thee in that fair Place,
  Where Light ſhall never fade.

Hail! Very Body of the Lord,
Who, man's Salvation to afford,
  Didſt hang upon the Tree;
Oh, ſave us from the pains of hell,
Moſt High Creator, Who doſt dwell
  A Prieſt eternally.

Hail! Jesu, hail! O living Bread,
Whereon our fainting Souls are fed,
 Both Truth and Way Thou art;
Be present now, to heal and bless,
And in Thy perfect Holiness
 Give us to have our part.

Hail! Banquet of the Angel Host,
Dear Solace of the tempest-tost,
 Who makest all things new;
Our earnest pleadings deign to hear,
Breathe on these hearts, so hard and sere,
 Thy Spirit's gracious Dew.

Hail! God, beneath this Veil concealed,
In Heaven all gloriously revealed,
 Where shadows flee away;
We pray Thee, shield us from our foe,
And give us once that Peace to know
 Which never can decay.

Hail! Sacred Drops of Jesu's Blood,
That open unto men the road
 High Heaven to attain;
Behold, O Lord, our sin we own,
Plead Thou before our Father's Throne,
 Our pardon to obtain.

Hail! Draught of Life, and Health, and Joy
All Sweetness that shall never cloy,
 All Virtue in Thee lies;

O Bleſſed CHRIST, be Merciful,
  Grant us forgiveneſs free and full,
    Who, Dead, for us didſt riſe.

Hail! Heavenly Splendour, WORD of GOD,
Flower and Fruit of Aaron's Rod,
    Thou Finger of the LORD,
Oh, let us not be caſt away;
Where Thou art throned in endleſs day,
    A place to us afford.

Hail! Sacred FLESH of CHRIST, that bore
All Agony and Paſſion ſore
    To ſhield us from our ſin;
Thou with the wicked mad'ſt Thy Grave,
Dear LORD, our ſinful Souls to ſave,
    And Heaven for us to win.

Manna moſt hidden, moſt Divine,
Upon us bid Thy Mercy ſhine,
    Oh, hear Thy Saints' deſire;
Set us, abſolved and purified,
And bleſſed and crowned and glorified,
    Amid th' Angelic Choir.

The Fountain of Life.

Whosoever drinketh of the Water that I shall give him,
shall never thirst.

 DROOP—oh, give me of the crystal
     Stream
     Which flows in ever-blooming Ama-
       ranth bowers;
The Fount immortal, whose transparent waves
   Reflect bright Angel faces 'midst the flowers;
     That fairest Stream o'erflows with Wisdom's
       richest ore—
     Oh, waft one priceless Drop, and Strength for
       evermore.

I droop—sustain me, blessed Fount of Life;
   Bid deepening shadows of the night depart;
Give Peace and Courage to the wavering mind,
   And Faith and Hope unto the sinking heart.
     O blessed, fragrant River, o'er the weary head
     May guardian Angel hands one Drop pel-
       lucid shed.

I droop—Redeemer, only Fount of Joy,
   From Thee alone the living Waters flow;
Give one sweet Drop to cool life's burning pain,
   There is no healing spring on earth below:
     They search in vain for aid, who search for
      aught but Thee,
     Thou art the Way, the Truth, in all Eternity.

The Reward of Perseverance.

*Sæpe corde tepido et arido accedimus, ad Altare
incumbimus.*

OFT when with icy heart, and dry
Affection's cold and tearless eye,
Barren as a desert, chilled as steel,
We at God's holy Altar kneel—
Still, while we persevere, and bear
With firm resolve, th' unlively prayer,
To holy sufferance will come
An Answer from our Heavenly home.

For oft amid the weary crush,
The springs of Grace, with sudden rush,
Will overspread the rocky breast
With verdure new and dews of rest,
Filling the longing heart's distress
With floods of love and happiness,
One draft of which will countervail
Long days of want, and nights of wail.

Ah, ye who sit beneath the cloud,
And mourn for absence, deep, not loud,
Know this, that he who meekly bows—
And silent, grieves his absent Spouse—
One unexpected day shall feel
How good it was for him to kneel,

And mourn a temporary loſs,
Under the ſhadow of the Croſs.

For ah, what words of beſt deſire,
What eloquence or Angel fire,
May tell the length, or breadth, or height,
The richneſs of extreme Delight,
Reſerved for him, who meekly bends,
Rather for Love, than lively ends,
Who, unrequited, perſeveres,
And labours ſtill, albeit in tears.

The Prieſt and the Altar.

Jam ſatis fluxit cruor hoſtiarum.

ENOUGH the blood of victims flowed of
      old,
    The ſhadows paſs, and legal offer-
      ings;
Now higher Miniſtries, Thou, LORD, doſt mould,
  On which a holier ſhade Thy Prieſthood flings.

Elias from the Heavens called down the flame;
  One Greater than Elias, hid from ſight,
Is here, obedient to His awful Name;
  Of Him we make the dread memorial Rite.

Great Office, the myſterious Cup to bear,
  In which the guilty world's Salvation lies,

And with our trembling hands, full of deep fear,
  To offer up the Bloodlefs Sacrifice.

Oh, more than all to ancient Prophets given,
  More than to Angels, if but underftood,
That in our trembling hands the GOD of Heaven
  Doth give Himfelf to be our Spirits' Food.

Grant, CHRIST, that we, fulfilling Thy Commands,
  Of Thy bleft Prefence may approach the Seat,
With hearts by Thee made pure, and holy hands;
  May Love for Thy dread Altars make us meet.

SON of th' Eternal FATHER, GOD above,
  May all the world beneath Thy Feet adore,
Who fendeft down the SPIRIT, with Thy Love
  Thy Priefthood to anoint for evermore.

𝕯𝖍𝖊 𝕭𝖑𝖊𝖘𝖘𝖊𝖉 𝕾𝖆𝖈𝖗𝖆𝖒𝖊𝖓𝖙.

Our GOD is a confuming Fire.

JESUS, Who for us haft died,
  The BLOOD flows ever from Thy Side,
For Thou art ever crucified,
      O burning Love.

By Prieftly hands Thy BLOOD is poured,
Upon the Altar, long and broad,
Where Thou art evermore ardored,
      O burning Love.

And on that Altar, day by day,
Thy Love holds on its ſhining way,
And ſheds an ever brightening ray,
      O burning Love.

Thy Sacrifice can never ceaſe,
'Till all is reſt, and joy, and peace,
In the triumphant world of Grace,
      O burning Love.

And on the Altar is our Food,
Purchaſed for us, by Thine Own BLOOD,
When Mary by the Croſs once ſtood ;
      O burning Love.

Thouſands of faithful hearts adore,
Where Thou art ſhrined for evermore,
A Beacon on a ſtormy ſhore,
      O burning Love.

Thy Tabernacle's ſun goes down,
When each Elect has won his Crown,
And all Thy mighty Love is ſhown,
      O burning Love.

Then, not till then, that burning Light
Goes down beneath the waters bright,
But there is Day, and no more night,
      O ever burning, burning Love.

The two great Gifts of Chriſt.

This is My Body.
Behold thy Mother.

EHOLD thy Mother—from the Croſs
    He gave her—not to one alone :
  We are His Brethren ; unto us
    He gave a Mother, as to John.

Behold the greateſt Gift of Christ,
    Save That wherein Himself He gives,
The Wonder-working Euchariſt,
    Sole Life of each that truly lives.

Myſterious Bread, not joined and knit
    With him that eats, like mortal food ;
But, fire-like, joining him with It,
    And blending with the Church of God.

Mary ! from thee the Saviour took
    That Flesh He gives. The Mercies twain,
Like ſtreams of a divided brook,
    But ſeparate to meet again.

The Cross of Jesus, the Fount of All Blessing.

Crux Tua, Bone Jesu, *omnium Fons Benedictionum,*
omnium Gratiarum Causa.

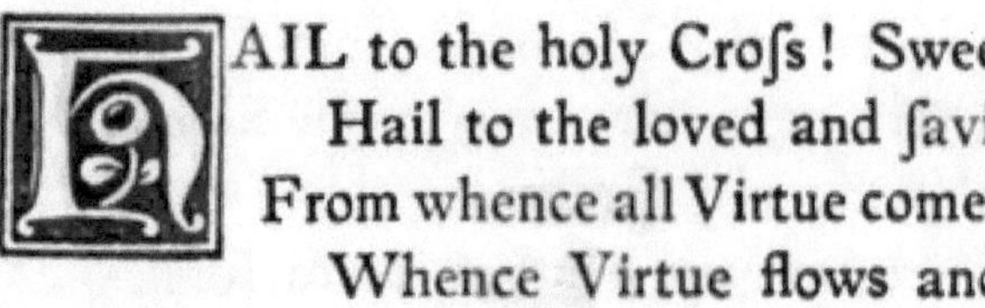AIL to the holy Cross! Sweet Jesus,
   Hail to the loved and saving Sign!
From whence all Virtue comes to ease us,
   Whence Virtue flows and Might
     Divine.

Hail to the Cross! Fount of all Blessings,
   Whence Grace descends in copious flood;
Worthy alone of all caressings,
   Hail to thee, loved and sacred Wood!

Hail to the holy Cross! that giveth
   Virtue, and Strength, and loving Faith;
Hail to the Cross! that ever liveth,
   Singing Life's triumph over death.

Hail to the Cross! from whence went raying,
   Athwart o'er earth, Love's holy flame;
Thy banner o'er its heights displaying,
   And reaping Glory from its shame.

Hail to the holy Cross! rejected
   Albeit, and scorned by worldly pride;
Yet by Almighty Love elected
   To be the meek and humble's guide.

Hail to the holy Cro∫s! affli&ion
  Sinks not the heart, nor bids it qualm ;
For thou, ∫weet Fount of Benedi&ion,
  Art near to pour the healing Balm.

Hail to thee, holy Cro∫s of ages !
  That bids attempered ∫orrow fall ;
Before thy foot, no tempe∫t rages,
  No ∫torms oppre∫s, no pa∫∫ions thrall.

Hail to the holy Cro∫s ! that bringe∫t
  From weakne∫s ∫trength, from ∫orrow, ea∫e ;
With more than eagle power that winge∫t
  Thy flight from earth to Heavenly Peace.

Hail ! Ark of Peace, on Thee confiding,
  Fierce winds may blow, wild waves may to∫s ;
For I am ∫afe, by thee abiding,
  Sweet JESUS, here, before Thy Face.

Hymn of the xib. Century.

CHRISTUS, *Lux indeficiens.*

CHRIST, the Light that knows no
        waning,
    Gives to us His FLESH as Food,
Drink He gives us al∫o, deigning
    To refre∫h us with His BLOOD.

CHRIST, Thou Radiance ever glowing,
  Who upon the Crofs didft bleed,
Light on all Thy Saints beftowing,
  With Thyfelf Thy Flock doft feed.

FLESH, Which we are now receiving,
  Of a Virgin took the WORD,
And the BLOOD we drink, believing
  He for finful man outpoured.

In this Rite, our Souls to nourifh,
  To the WORD made FLESH we come ;
Hence, our faith in ftrength doth flourifh ;
  Hence, we reach our Heavenly home.

Bread of Sweetnefs, ever holy,
  Full art Thou of pure Delight ;
SAVIOUR, born of Maiden lowly,
  King art Thou of perfe&ct; Might.

May we ever eat in gladnefs
  Of this rich, Angelic Bread ;
May we, in death's hour of fadnefs,
  With this fweeteft Gift be fed.

He was, at the third day-hour,
  Led a Vi&ct;im forth to die,
When He bare His Crofs of Power,
  His Ele&ct; to raife on high.

Lead us, Giver of Salvation,
  To our Home Thyfelf befide,

Where eternal Jubilation
  Dwelleth through the LAMB that died.

Evermore we there the ſtory
  Of Thy wondrous Deeds will raiſe,
Reigning with Thy Saints in Glory,
  We will offer gifts of praiſe.

Sacrifice and hymns in union,
  GOD, we bring this feſtal day ;
May He with Divine Communion
  Feed us in His Love for aye.

𝕿𝖍𝖊 𝖕𝖑𝖊𝖆𝖉𝖎𝖓𝖌 𝕻𝖗𝖊𝖘𝖊𝖓𝖈𝖊 𝖔𝖋 𝕮𝖍𝖗𝖎𝖘𝖙 𝖎𝖓 𝕳𝖊𝖆𝖛𝖊𝖓.

This MAN, *becauſe He continueth ever, hath an unchangeable Prieſthood.*

HAIL to GOD's True BODY !
    Of Virgin Mary ſprung,
  Truly for us offered,
    On Croſs of anguiſh hung,
Whoſe dear Side was truly
  By ſpear enforced to bleed ;
In our lateſt conflict
  Upon Thee let us feed.

Once for all, O JESU,
  Thou waſt a Victim made ;
Still in Heaven Thou pleadeſt,
  In FLESH and BLOOD diſplayed ;

But though round this Altar
   Nought of Heaven appear,
Thy ſtrong Word and Action
   Doth make Thee Preſent here.

In very Life and Eſſence
   Thou doſt Thy Word fulfil,
Who, whereſoe'er Thou liveſt,
   Art Mediator ſtill;
O qui peccata tollis,
   To Thee our greetings riſe—
All hail! the pleading Preſence,
   All hail! the Sacrifice.

The Bread becomes Thy BODY,
   The Wine becomes Thy BLOOD,
And both, O Love Incarnate,
   Are our Life-giving Food.
What Thou to GOD preſenteſt,
   To ſinners Thou doſt give,
So, bending to adore Thee,
   We eat, and drink, and live.

Prayer to Jeſus in the Bleſſed Sacrament.

*Remember me, O LORD, according to the Favour that
Thou beareſt unto Thy People.*

JESU CHRIST, remember,
   When Thou ſhalt come again,
Upon the clouds of Heaven,
   With all Thy ſhining Train;

When every eye ſhall ſee Thee
  In DEITY revealed
Who now upon this Altar
  In ſilence art concealed ;
Remember then, O SAVIOUR,
  I ſupplicate of Thee,
That here I bowed before Thee,
  Upon my bended knee ;
That here I owned Thy Preſence,
  And did not Thee deny,
And glorified Thy Greatneſs,
  Though hid from human eye.
Accept, Divine Redeemer,
  The homage of my praiſe ;
Be Thou the Light, and Honour,
  And Glory of my days.
Be Thou my Conſolation
  When death is drawing nigh ;
Be Thou my only Treaſure
  Through all Eternity.

A Sequence of the xvi. Century.

Ave ! CARO CHRISTI.

HOLY FLESH of CHRIST our King,
  Thee, Adorable, we ſing ;
  In the New Law's happy Vale,
  Paſture of the true Flock, hail !
Pure and ſpotleſs be the breaſt
Where Thou comeſt as the Gueſt ;

Let the Faithful hourly fay—
Thee we worfhip, Thee we pray.

Thee, the Church, Thy myftic Wife,
Worfhips as the BREAD of Life;
Ranfom, Guide, Redeemer, we
Covet bleft Satiety;
We, the finners, need Thy Balm;
We, the mourners, feek Thy Calm;
Bring us out of life's lorn road
Into Glory, unto GOD.

The Altar Shade.

A MAN *fhall be as a Covert from the tempeft, as the
Shadow of a great Rock in a weary land.*

ORTH from the dark and ftormy fky,
LORD, to Thine Altar fhade we fly;
Forth from the world, its hope and fear,
SAVIOUR, we feek Thy Shelter here;
Weary and weak, Thy Grace we pray;
Turn not, O LORD, Thy Guefts away.

Long have we roam'd in want and pain,
Long have we fought Thy Reft in vain;
Wildered in doubt, in darknefs loft,
Long have our Souls been tempeft-toft;
Low at Thy Feet our fins we lay;
Turn not, O LORD, Thy Guefts away.

An Ancient Act of Adoration.

CHRISTI CORPUS, *Ave!*

AIL! BODY, born of Mary,
    Hail! CHRIST, Redeemer dear,
True MAN and perfect GODHEAD
    And Living FLESH are here.

Hail! Thou, our true Salvation,
    The Way, the Life, art Thou,
With Thy Right Hand of Power
    Save us from evil now.

Hail! BLOOD of CHRIST, in Heaven
    The Chalice of the bleſt,
The Water of Redemption
    To cleanſe the ſinful breaſt.

Hail! BLOOD and ſaving Water,
    That from the wounded Side
Of CHRIST, our dear Redeemer,
    Flowed for us when He died.

An Euchariſtic Prayer.

JESU, *nobis miſerere.*

AIL! CHRIST's BODY, True and Real,
    Of the Virgin Mary born,
Truly ſuffering, truly offered
    On the Croſs and hill of ſcorn.

L

Hail! for man's Salvation pierced,
   Gaping Wounds, and riven Side,
Whence outflowed with Love unſtinting,
   Blood and Water, mingled Tide.
Now upon that Body feed we,
   And of that ſweet Fountain drink,
Leſt when death relentleſs ſeize us,
   'Neath the Judge's ſearch we ſink.

Loving, Gentle Son of Mary,
Never of our pardon weary,
Jesu, nobis miſerere.
Grant that as I ſee Thee now
   Veiled beneath the Form of Bread,
When Thou com'ſt the Heaven to bow,
   And to judge the quick and dead,
Freed by Thee from every fear,
   I may then lift up my head,
Glad to know and ſee Thee near.

Hail! O Flesh of Christ, the Victim
   On the Altar of the Croſs,
Offered to the Father's Juſtice,
   Suff'ring to redeem our loſs.
By Thy bitter Death redeemèd,
   May we all Thy Brightneſs ſee;
Grant us glorious fruition
   Of eternal Joy with Thee.
Hail! Thou Word of God Incarnate,
   On Thine Altar Thee we ſeek,
Thee the loving Bread of Angels,
   Health and Hope to ſick and weak.

Jesu, hail! from Heaven defcending,
On the Crofs Thine Arms extending,
Healing fin, and forrow ending.
Thou of Goodnefs infinite,
    Fount of Pity, Loving LORD,
Sinners' Hope, and Saints' Delight,
    Angels' Praife, Thy Grace accord :
Of our pardon never weary,
JESU, nobis miferere.

Thoughts upon the Real Presence.

*The Cup of Blefing which we blefs, is It not the Com-
munion of the* BLOOD *of* CHRIST *? The Bread which
we break, is It not the Communion of the* BODY *of*
CHRIST *?*

TAKE, GOD, Thine own, thefe Gifts are
            Thine
        We to Thy holy Altar bring ;
    Yet deign'ft Thou in Thy Love Divine
To take them as man's offering :
Take then Thine own, for all are Thine—
Thefe poor Oblations of our Bread and Wine.

Thou that haft gained again Thine Home,
    Abandoned once for man to die,
Come in Thy facred Prefence, come,
    Clothed in an awful Myftery ;
Thy facred Boon of mighty Love prefent,
Veiled in its Sacramental Element.

Come, as Thy Truth hath ſaid Thou wilt,
　The Food of Life to give ;
Thy BLOOD, Thy BODY, broken, ſpilt,
　That dying man may live :
SAVIOUR, to us Thy Love extend ;
JESUS, Bleſt Victim of the world, deſcend.

Bow down ; the conſecrating hand
　The myſtic Bread hath broken ;
Moved by the Power of GOD's Command,
　The Bleſſing hath been ſpoken :
Bow down, bow down, thy GOD revere ;
Veiled in this broken Form, Thy GOD is here.

Bow down, the hallowed Wine is reared,
　Bleſt into Life, with Life It flows ;
A SAVIOUR from the ſins we feared,
　A Strength and Healer of our woes :
Bow down, in this bleſt Symbol lies
My SAVIOUR's BLOOD, Earth's bleeding Sacrifice.

Come, HOLY GHOST, my Soul fulfil
　With faith to hold this Myſtery ;
Unchanged to ſight, yet bear they ſtill
　The Very GOD's Humanity :
Faith aſks not how, but graſps GOD's Word,
As faultleſs Truth to mortal ſenſe preferred.

Why ſeek to know what GOD hath ſealed ?
　Faith were an empty ſound,

If nought but what our fight revealed
　　Around our courfe were found—
LORD, I believe ; increafe my faith
To take on truft whate'er the SPIRIT faith.

Come Faith, and fit me to receive
　　This facred Food whereon I feed ;
So may the Prefence of His BODY give
　　Onenefs and fellowfhip indeed ;
I joined in CHRIST, and CHRIST in me,
A true Communion—yet a Myftery.

Joined to His BODY, may my body prove
　　A worthier member of my facred Head ;
May the rich Drops of BLOOD remove
　　The ftains I loathe, the wrath I dread :
Grant that my body and my Soul may find
Their portion, in the SAVIOUR of mankind.

A Sequence on the Precious Blood, of the xbi. Century.

Reminifcens Beati SANGUINIS.

ROM their hid fpring my tears are
　　　falling,
　　My heart the Bleffed BLOOD recalling,
　　Which man's Creator poured for me
In lavifh torrents from the Tree ;
It is a Stream of fuch Delight
That none who taftes fhould ill requite.

Why doſt Thou ſuffer woes ſo many,
Sweet Jesu? Sins Thou didſt not any;
By Thee came never crime's offence,
Thou art the Flower of Innocence:
Thine is the ſcourge, the robber I;
I am the guilty, Thou doſt die.

Why for the worthleſs, Price ſo great?
Is it for earthly wealth or ſtate?
Oh, Thou hadſt Glory none may ſhare,
None can approach it, none declare;
Yet with ſuch Love Thy Heart did flame,
It made the ſhameful Croſs no ſhame.

If ne'er for what Thy Grace has given
A praiſeful anſwer mounts to Heaven,
If ne'er with love for Love I burn,
Nor to Thy Sorrows make return
In labours dear to God through Thee,
Woe to the wretched, woe to me.

Oh, can I ſee Thee ſtretched on high
In holieſt death-throes, yet paſs by?
Oh, can I live for ought elſe now
My little life-ſpace? I do vow
To Thee, an offering utter, whole,
My two-fold being, fleſh and Soul.

Ye, who are now far off, oh, fly
Unto the ſweet Croſs, leſt ye die;

Ye, who now live to ſelf, oh, ſtrive
That ye may live to GOD, and live :
Would ye be members reckonèd ?
Ye muſt be pierced, as was your Head.

Oh, look not on that Streaming BLOOD
With eyes of cold ingratitude ;
Let there be tears and mighty crying,
Your GOD upon the Croſs is dying ;
And love and grief to Him are due
Who loved and grieved to BLOOD for you.

Lo, He has bought a Kingdom bleſt,
And ſet for man a Port of reſt ;
No key can ope that Kingdom's door,
No ſhip can reach the happy Shore,
Except amain they faſhioned be
Of nails and wood from Calvary.

Hail, BLOOD ! Which quickeneſt man within,
And, ſtreaming, bid'ſt him enter in :
If any ſin-ſtain foul my Soul,
In Mercy waſh me, make me whole ;
And till I go hence, each new want
With new-born Bounty heed, and grant.

PART IV.

THE COMMUNION.

The Soul's Invitation to Holy Communion.

Come, for all things are now ready.

THE Board is ſpread with Meats
Divine,
O worn with ſtrife, and ſoiled
with ſin,
Draw near, love-thirſting Soul of
mine,
Draw near, and take thy SAVIOUR in.

I ſee the white preparèd Board,
I hear the words of Love and Grace,
But canſt Thou deign to dwell, O LORD,
Within ſo foul and ſoiled a place?

Fair was the shrine the Prophet-chief
  Made for Thy Dwelling-place of old,
With curtain fine, and Almond leaf,
  And Shittim shaft, and ring of gold.

More fair on green Moriah's breast
  The House the Monarch reared for Thee,
With costly gems, and odours drest,
  With burning lamp, and molten sea,

With Cedar flower, and carven Palm,
  In purest gold of Parvaim set,
And pillars hung, like ships a-calm,
  Each spell-bound in its gilded net.

Poor heart; ah, where thy hallowed fires?
  Thy gold of consecrated days,
The broidered veil of pure desires,
  The cedar-scented songs of praise?

A nobler hand to grace Thy shrine,
  Gems of more wondrous beauty brought,
Gave all the reasoning powers Divine,
  The light of Love, the wealth of thought.

Ah, me! the world has come between
  Thy Soul and CHRIST; the gold is dim,
The floor is soiled He made so clean;
  Is this a dwelling fit for Him?

Yet, come; I see the Wine, the Bread;
    That BLOOD can wash away thy sin;
Draw near, my Soul, and be thou fed,
    Nor doubt, but CHRIST will enter in.

Hymn of S. Thomas Aquinas.

VERBUM *Supernum prodiens.*

THE Heavenly WORD proceeding forth,
    Yet leaving not the FATHER's Side,
Accomplishing His Work on earth,
    Had reached at length life's eventide
By false Disciple to be given
    To foemen for His Life athirst,
Himself the very Bread of Heaven,
    He gave to His Disciples first.

He gave Himself in either Kind,
    His Precious FLESH, His Precious BLOOD,
In Love's own fulness thus designed
    Of the whole man to be the Food.
By birth their Fellow-man was He;
    Their Meat, when sitting at the board;
He died their Ransomer to be;
    He ever reigns, their great Reward.

O Saving Victim, opening wide
    The gate of Heaven to man below;
Our foes press on from every side,
    Thine Aid supply, Thy Strength bestow.

Bleſt THREE in ONE, to Thee aſcend
　All Thanks and Praiſe for evermore,
Oh, grant us Life that ſhall not end
　Upon the Heavenly Country's ſhore.

𝕳𝖞𝖒𝖓 𝖔𝖋 𝖙𝖍𝖊 𝕳𝖔𝖑𝖞 𝕱𝖊𝖆𝖘𝖙.

I am That BREAD *of Life.*

KING of Beauty, LORD of Love,
　True Bread and living Stay,
How doſt Thou ſweet Refreſhment
　　prove
To pilgrims on their way.

O precious Drops, that from yon Fount
　Of Comfort ever flow,
Who taſte of Theſe all toil ſurmount,
　They ſweeten every woe.

Manna Celeſtial daily ſpread,
　Drink from the Rock outpoured,
Thus through the wild are nouriſhed
　Thy ſorrowing Children, LORD.

Thrice bleſſed they, who day by day
　On JESU's Breaſt recline;
With Thee, indeed, no more we need,
　Who giv'ſt Thyſelf to Thine.

Self-Searching at Communion.

Stretch forth thine hand.

LORD, at this moment Thou art surely
here,
And I Thy Presence feel;
I feel Thy pitying Eye bend o'er my
head,
I hear Thy gentle Footsteps near me tread,
And at Thy Feet I kneel.

I kneel; I tell Thee all my inmost woe,
Tell of a load of sin;
I ask Thy Pity, Pardon, and Relief;
I shew Thee all my bitter, bitter grief,
The deep distress within.

I count my years, to Thee, a wasted life
With so much left undone,
It looks so sad, now Thou Thyself art near,
Thy Human Life shines out so pure and clear,
And mine in sin has run.

Now, while I see Thy Wounds—I feel it all—
Too much for me to bear:
I need to draw new Life in every breath;
I need a Rescue in the hour of death,
And One my griefs to share.

And while I lay this sadness at Thy Feet,
I feel Thee nearing me—

Stretch forth thine hand—I know Thy healing
    Voice ;
It makes this weary, mournful heart rejoice,
    And draws me nearer Thee,

Nearer and nearer ſtill ; gives me Thyſelf
    In wondrous Myſtery ;
Unites me with Thee, and Thyſelf with me,
In ſorrow, joy, through life, through death, to be
    Thine in Eternity.

The Type and Antitype of the Bleſſed Sacrament.

Hoſte dum victo triumphans.

WHEN the Patriarch was returning
    Crown'd with triumph from the
      fray,
    Him the peaceful King of Salem
Came to meet upon his way,
Meekly bearing Bread and Wine,
Holy Prieſthood's awful Sign.

On the Truth, thus dimly ſhadowed,
    Later days a luſtre ſhed ;
When the great High Prieſt Eternal,
    Under Forms of Wine and Bread,
    For the world's immortal Food,
    Gave His FLESH and gave His BLOOD.

Wondrous Gift—The WORD who moulded
    All things by His Might Divine,

Bread into His Body changes,
   Into His Own Blood the Wine ;
   What though ſenſe no change perceives,
   Faith admires, adores, believes.

He Who once to die a Victim
   On the Croſs, did not refuſe,
Day by day, upon our Altars,
   That ſame Sacrifice renews ;
   Through His holy Prieſthood's hands,
   Faithful to His laſt Commands.

While the people all uniting
   In the Sacrifice ſublime,
Offer CHRIST to His High FATHER,
   Offer up themſelves with Him ;
   Then, together with the Prieſt,
   On the Living Victim feaſt.

An Euchariſtic Prayer.

To know the Love of CHRIST *which paſſeth knowledge.*

ESU, to Thy Table led,
   Now let every heart be fed
   With the true and living Bread.

While in penitence we kneel,
   Thy ſweet Preſence let us feel,
   All Thy wondrous Love reveal.

While on Thy dear Crofs we gaze,
Mourning o'er our finful ways,
Turn our fadnefs into praife.

Draw us to Thy wounded Side,
Whence there flowed the healing Tide ;
There our fins and forrows hide.

From the bonds of fin releafe,
Cold and wavering faith increafe,
LAMB of GOD, grant us Thy Peace.

Lead us by Thy piercèd Hand,
Till around Thy Throne we ftand,
In the bright and better Land.

Union with Christ in Holy Communion.

My Beloved is Mine, and I am His.

ONE holds me faft : kept in His pure
            Embrace
                I reft in peace :
        Flows on my weary heart His foftening
            Grace,
    And troubles ceafe.

Though cold the ftorm, and fierce the blafting wind,
        I do not fear,
For in His Breaft a Covert fafe I find :
        No ftorm comes there.

He ſhields me tenderly—my Spouſe, my Love—
    He guides me on
To Manſions fair, prepared for me above,
    Where He has gone.

He feeds me, leſt I faint, or fall, or die,
    With Food from Heaven :
He, His Own SELF, in wondrous Myſtery
    To me has given.

He draws me to Himſelf; I needs muſt go ;
    I cannot ſtay :
No earthly tie muſt bind me here below :
    But far away,

Where, 'mid the countleſs throngs of Angels bright
    And Spirits bleſt,
He reigns—my GOD and King—my ſole Delight,
    I long to reſt.

An Ancient Proſe on the Sacrament of the Altar.

Panis deſcendens Cœlitus.

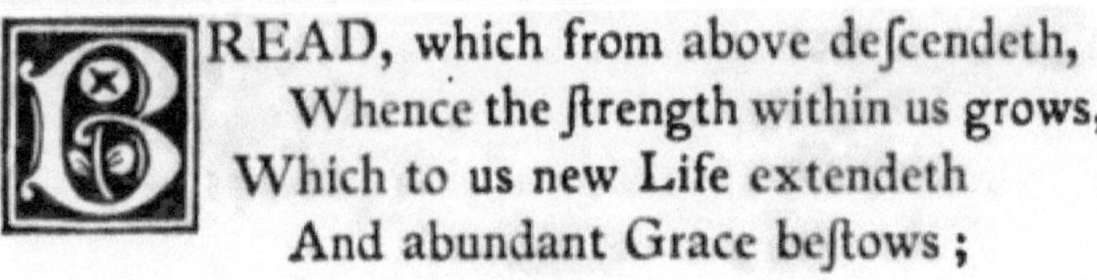

BREAD, which from above deſcendeth,
    Whence the ſtrength within us grows,
    Which to us new Life extendeth
    And abundant Grace beſtows ;

May CHRIST be that Feaſt unto us
  Which true Nouriſhment imparts,
And the Cup which doth renew us,
  Filling full of Joy our hearts.

Splendour of the Light of Heaven
  Whom unceaſing praiſes greet,
As at Thy Laſt Supper given,
  Give us of Thy FLESH to eat.

Heavenly Banquet of the living,
  Glory in Redemption ſhown,
Reſt unto the humble giving,
  Make the Bliſs of Heaven our own.

To the Memory ſtill returning
  Of Thy Death for us accurſt,
Snatch us from the Lake of burning,
  Thou, Who didſt exclaim—I thirſt.

LORD, to Thee Thy Church gives honour
  For Thy countleſs Bleſſings all;
Pour Thy Gracious Light upon her,
  Both in Faſt and Feſtival.

With the SON and HOLY SPIRIT,
  ˙ GOD the FATHER, ever Bleſt,
May we by the Gifts inherit
  Of this Feaſt eternal Reſt.

Eucharistic Colloquy.

O Jesu, du mein Brautigam.

ORD Jesu, Bridegroom of my Soul,
Make me, Thy humble servant, whole,
By that Dear Blood which on the Crofs
Thou fheddeft to redeem man's lofs.

Full of defire, yet full of fear,
To Thine own Altar I draw near,
And though my fteps have gone aftray,
In Mercy caft me not away.

O Thou good Shepherd of Thy Flock,
My King, my Lord, my Spoufe, my Rock,
Who haft o'er fin the vict'ry won,
Put me the Wedding Garment on.

Cure, great Phyfician, my difeafe,
And heal mine oft infirmities ;
Wafh every finful ftain away,
And let me tafte Thyfelf to-day.

Though oft in finfulnefs laid low,
Thy pard'ning Love on me beftow,
And mortify my proud felf-love,
And let Thy Grace my Glory prove.

To thoſe who fight in ſin's dread ſtrife
Thy BODY is the Bread of Life,
Thy BLOOD the Wine Divine of Love,
The richeſt from Thy Stores above.

Hungry and thirſty, lo, I come,
Oh, find me at Thy Table room;
To me of this bleſt Banquet give,
And let me eat, and drink, and live.

Take from my heart each thought of ſin,
And let Thy SPIRIT enter in;
Grant Faith, and Hope, and bleſſed Love,
Gifts of Thy SPIRIT from above.

What Soul and body need, ſupply;
Remove what's hurtful to Thine Eye;
Dwell in my heart, and let me be
In ſweeteſt Union, LORD, with Thee.

Againſt my Soul, when earth or Hell
Combine, or mine own heart rebel,
Subdue my foes, my heart ſubdue,
And keep me to Thy Service true.

Adorn my converſation, LORD,
With all the Graces of Thy Word,
And do Thou grant me all my days
To keep Thy Law and ſing Thy praiſe;

That when, O gracious Prince of Life,
Thou call'ſt me from this world of ſtrife,
I may to Thy bleſt Preſence riſe,
And live with Thee above the ſkies.

𝔄 𝔖𝔢𝔮𝔲𝔢𝔫𝔠𝔢 𝔬𝔣 𝔱𝔥𝔢 𝔵𝔳𝔦. 𝔆𝔢𝔫𝔱𝔲𝔯𝔶.

De Supernâ Hierarchiâ.

FROM the moſt holy Place above,
    In the world's latter day,
    The Wiſdom true of GOD came down
        To guide us on our way;
Oh, we had ever longed for Him,
    And He at laſt was given,
Mary the Virgin's Bleſſed CHILD,
    JESUS, the mortal's Haven.

Great was He ever; great the name
    The Holy Virgin won,
When by a Miracle ſhe roſe
    Mother to ſuch a SON;
He takes this loſt world's ſin away,
    Forward with Might He goes,
And in the van of fainting men
    Doth put to flight their foes.

There was no ſorrow in His Home,
    There was no death on High,
He ſought Him FLESH to ſorrow in,
    A Croſs, that He might die;

He is the righteous Lawgiver,
  And yet Himself He gave
Unto the Law's most bitter scourge,
  Us from its curse to save.

For lo! the LAMB was lifted up
  Upon the cruel Tree,
And He was sacrificed for us,
  Incarnate Charity;
Thus our marred life was built again—
  Upon each infant brow
The Sign of Him who saves is set,
  And Heaven is open now.

It was the night He was betrayed,
  When in an Upper Room
With His loved Twelve He sat at meat,
  Knowing what soon should come:
He blessed and brake the Holy Bread
  And said—O hearken ye
Who doubt Him—This My BODY is;
  Do this, remembering Me.

He ceased. Anon, He spake again,
  GOD's Holy SON and True,
And thus the Gift unspeakable
  Came in the Chalice too;
It had made glad man's heavy heart,
  But then His All It stood,
The Drink of the new Paradise,
  The WORD Incarnate's BLOOD.

This Myſtery is hid in GOD,
    This can none elſe explore,
Be Thou content to wait awhile,
    Believe, embrace, adore;
But be thou ware to eat and drink,
    If ſlave to ſin thou be,
Only the pure and guileleſs heart
    Can take It worthily.

Say, canſt thou love as Peter loved?
    Behold thy Peace is here;
Art thou a Judas? in thy ſins
    Come not, O traitor, near;
This is the juſt man's aliment,
    This arms him for the fray;
But whoſo lacks a Wedding robe
    Is the Foe's certain prey.

Thine is this Marvel, Bleſſed CHRIST,
    Thine would Its ſharers be;
Oh, ſave us from eternal Wrath,
    Clothe us with chaſtity:
Thou haſt reſtored the breach; to Thee
    For Health and Peace we come;
Make us more worthy of Thy Gift,
    Bring us more near our Home.

Conference between Christ, the Saints, and the Soul.

Come up hither, and I will shew thee things which must be hereafter.

 AM pale with fick defire,
 For my heart is far away
From this world's fitful fire
 And this world's waning day :
In a dream it overleaps
 A world of tedious ills
To where the funfhine fleeps
 On th' everlafting hills.
 Say the Saints—There Angels eafe us,
  Glorified and white.
 They fay—We reft in JESUS,
  Where is not day nor night.

My Soul faith—I have fought
 For a home that is not gained ;
I have fpent, yet nothing bought ;
 Have laboured, but not attained :
My pride ftrove to rife and grow,
 And hath but dwindled down ;
My love fought love, and lo,
 Hath not attained its crown.
 Say the Saints—Frefh Souls increafe us,
  None languifh or recede.

They ſay—We love our Jesus,
   And He loves us indeed.

I cannot riſe above,
   I cannot reſt beneath,
I cannot find out love,
   Or eſcape from death :
Dear hopes and joys gone by
   Still mock me with a name,
My beſt belovèd die
    And I cannot die with them.
    Say the Saints—No deaths decreaſe us,
      Where our reſt is glorious.
    They ſay—We live in Jesus,
     Who once dièd for us.

Oh, my Soul, ſhe beats her wings
   And pants to fly away
Up to immortal things
   In the Heavenly day :
Yet ſhe flags and almoſt faints ;
   Can ſuch be meant for me ?
Come and ſee—ſay the Saints.
    Saith Jesus—Come and ſee.
    Say the Saints—His Pleaſures pleaſe us
      Before God and the Lamb.
    Come and taſte My ſweets—ſaith Jeſus—
     Be with Me where I am.

Eucharistic Prayer, of the xv. Century.

O Colenda Deitas.

GLORIOUS Object of our praiſe,
 Bleſſed Fount of our ſupply,
While in faith our voice we raiſe,
 Look on us, and hear our cry:
Open here the glorious Heaven,
 Where Thy Majeſty is known ;
Now let living Light be given
 From the Splendour of Thy Throne.
Viſit us, and make us ſee
 Thy Salvation here below ;
Till, preſented unto Thee,
 We ſhall all its Sweetneſs know.

Fill our hearts with Heavenly Love ;
 Make us rich and flouriſhing ;
Let Thy Spirit from above
 His enkindling Influence bring :
Show the riches of Thy Grace ;
 Rain the ſacred Manna down ;
Make us one in Thy Embrace ;
 Let Thy Love the Union crown.
Ever-bleſſed God, behold
 Not the vileneſs of our ſtate ;
But how Good Thou art unfold,
 And how mercifully Great.

Though defpifed, we look to Thee;
  Deign to hear our earneft cry;
Let us Thy fweet Mercy fee;
  Give us, LORD, a large fupply.
DEITY, Supreme o'er all,
  Condefcend to fhow Thy Love;
While before Thy Feet we fall,
  Pour Thy Bleffing from above.
Praife we give Thee, Glorious LORD,
  Singing with the Heavenly Hoft,
Now and ever be adored,
    FATHER, SON, and HOLY GHOST.

The hidden Altar=Life.

Verily, Thou art a GOD *that hideſt Thyſelf.*

O JESU, it was furely fweet,
  To fit and liften at Thy Feet,
  With thofe who in Thy Life drew near,
  Thy Words of Love and Grace to hear.

And fweet it was to walk with Thee,
Befide the lake of Galilee;
Or, fafe embarked in Peter's Boat,
O'er its blue waves with Thee to float.

But fweeter far it is to pray
Before Thine Altar-throne to-day,
For there th' atoning Sacrifice,
JESUS, the world's Redeemer, lies.

Hail! JESUS, hail! my Deareſt LORD,
By Seraph-choirs in Heaven adored;
Hail! JESUS, Who art Hidden thus
On this poor earth for Love of us.

Anima Christi.

Thou art a Place to hide me in.

SOUL of JESUS—once for me
Offered on the ſhameful Tree,
Heal, and make me by that Cure
Pure, as Thou Thyſelf art Pure;
Thou of Life the Fountain fair,
Draw me in, and keep me there.

Form of JESUS—ONE with GOD,
Who the dreadful winepreſs trod,
Man of Sorrows, drowned in grief,
Thou of ſin the ſole Relief,
Be Thy Sacramental Power
Preſent at my dying hour.

Holy JESUS, Great I AM,
Shining in a Spotleſs LAMB,
Gentle as the Heavenly DOVE,
Thou the LORD of Light and Love,
By Thy Paſſion, by Thy Prayer,
Snatch me from my own deſpair.

Hide me where that Wound was given,
Piercing to the Heart of Heaven;
Hide me where thoſe nails unmeet
Rent Thy Hands, and fixed Thy Feet;
Hide me where red Drops ran down
From that ſad acanthine Crown.

Blood of Jesus—crimſon Sea,
Glorious as eternity,
Fathomleſs, alone, ſublime,
Boundleſs Bath of human crime,
Me the leper, vile and mean,
Plunge me there, and make me clean.

Water—from that ſacred Side
Of a God, who groaned and died,
Blending with the purple Gore
When His Agony was o'er,
Flow in Mercy, full and free,
Flow for ſinners, flow for me.

Holy Jesus—let me be
Never ſeparate from Thee;
From the malice of the foe,
Ward me in the vale of woe;
Let me, yielding up my breath,
Find a Paradiſe in death.

There no more ſhall night be known,
Safely proſtrate at Thy Throne;

Called by Thee to realms of day
Where all tears are wiped away,
Jesu, Thou my Reſt ſhalt be,
Faith hath found her home in Thee.

The Marriage Supper of the Lamb.

Heil'ger Tiſch den Jesus *decket.*

THIS holy Feaſt, by Jesus ſpread,
Makes glad, yet fills my Soul with dread,
    Such conflict who can quell?
  We eat for better or for worſe;
I ſee before me, Bleſſing, curſe—
    Life, death—or Heaven, or Hell.

Yet, Lord, I come.   Thou doſt invite;
But firſt befitting Robe of white
    With jealous care put on;
While I by faith my heart prepare,
And ſo that feſtal Garment wear,
    Which Thou Thyſelf haſt won.

O Friend, among ten thouſand chief,
Good Shepherd, bring me quick relief,
    My faltering footſteps ſtay;
Set free my limbs, for I am bound;
Heal me, I have a deadly wound;
    Lead me, I've gone aſtray.

My thirſt and hunger let me ſlake,
And freely Life's pure Waters take,
   Thou, Whom my Soul doth prize;
Oh, ſave me, ſunk in grievous plight;
I grope in darkneſs, give me Light,
   Give Life to one who dies.

O. LORD, with rigour chide not one
Who ſuppliant comes before Thy Throne,
   Spurn not in Anger fierce;
With heart and knee before Thee bowed,
Let this my prayer pierce through the cloud,
   To Thy bright Preſence pierce.

LORD, let Thy FLESH, Which in my ſtead
Once bore the Croſs, be now my Bread;
   And Thy moſt Precious BLOOD—
Let not that Stream have flowed in vain,
But let theſe Both my ſtrength ſuſtain,
   And be my Higheſt Good.

An Ancient Anthem.

O Eſca viatorum.

FOOD that weary pilgrims love,
O Bread of Angel Hoſts above,
   O Manna of the Saints,
   The hungry Soul would feed on Thee;
Ne'er may the heart unſolaced be
Which for Thy Sweetneſs faints.

O Fount of Love, O cleanſing Tide,
Which from the SAVIOUR's pierced Side
    And ſacred Heart doſt flow,
Be ours to drink of Thy pure Rill,
Which only can our Spirits fill,
    And all we need beſtow.

O JESU, Whom, by Power Divine
Now hidden 'neath the outward Sign,
    We worſhip and adore,
Grant, when the veil away is rolled,
With open Face we may behold
    Thyſelf for evermore.

The Angel's Invitation to the Prophet.

*An Angel touched him, and ſaid unto him——Ariſe
and eat.*

CHRISTIAN, did no one, thinkeſt thou,
        behold thee,
        What time thou fainted'ſt in the noon-
        day heat?
Heard'ſt thou no Angel's voice, which ſweetly told
    thee——
    The journey is too great ; Ariſe and eat.

An Angel's voice? Nay, 'twas thy GOD that
        ſpake it,
    In fonder tones than Angel could repeat :

Himſelf the Food, His own the Hands that
　　brake It ;
　　His own the Words that bade thee—Riſe
　　and eat :

This is the Bread of Life which came from Heaven,
　　And now for thee is on My Table ſpread :
This is My BODY, Which for Thee was given ;
　　And this My BLOOD, Which for thy ſins was
　　ſhed.

Oh, fainting, faltering wanderer, art thou able
　　Still to refuſe thy Suppliant GOD's Requeſt ?—
Be filled, ye hungry, from My bounteous Table ;
　　And come, ye weary, I will give you reſt.

Oh, may His gracious, oft-urged Invitation
　　Subdue thee with its tones ſo ſoft and ſweet ;
Mayſt thou, at length, with heartfelt adoration
　　And tearful penitence—Ariſe and eat.

Another Banquet is for thee preparing ;
　　Another Feaſt thy longing eyes ſhall greet ;
An Angel's voice ſhall break thy reſt, declaring—
　　Behold, all things are ready ; Riſe and eat.

Eucbariſtic Antbem ; from tbe German.

Behold the LAMB *of* GOD.

B EHOLD the LORD,
　Th' Incarnate WORD,
　Our Higheſt Good,
　The Angels' Food,

Confents to reft
Within thy breaft :
  Bleffed JESU, we adore Thee
  In this Thy Holy Sacrament.

His Might He fhrouds
Beneath the Clouds
  Of Bread and Wine :
  This lowly Shrine
Contains the King
Whom Angels fing :
  Bleffed JESU, we adore Thee
  In this Thy Holy Sacrament.

Bow heart and knee,
GOD is with Thee ;
  Oh, truft and love—
  CHRIST from above
Will dry thy tears
And hufh thy fears :
  Bleffed JESU, we adore Thee
  In this Thy Holy Sacrament.

The Great I AM,
The Pafchal LAMB,
  Who fhed the Flood
  Of Precious BLOOD,
Lo ! here He lies
Our Sacrifice ;
  Bleffed JESU, we adore Thee
  In this Thy Holy Sacrament.

He calleth thee—
Come unto Me,
　　Thy pain and grief
　　Shall find relief;
Oh, come and hide
In My pierced Side :
　　Bleſſed Jesu, we adore Thee
　　In this Thy Holy Sacrament.

Lord, come at laſt
When life is paſt,
　　In my laſt hour,
　　With Love and Power,
To be my Light
Through death's dark night :
　　Bleſſed Jesu, we adore Thee
　　In this Thy Holy Sacrament.

A Prayer to the Lord Jesus.

He was wounded for our tranſgreſſions ; He was bruiſed
for our iniquities.

JESUS, bruiſed and wounded more
　　Than burſted grape, or bread of wheat,
The Life of Life within our Souls,
　　The Cup of our Salvation ſweet,
We come to ſhow Thy dying Hour,
Thy ſtreaming Vein, Thy Broken Flesh ;

And ſtill the BLOOD is warm to ſave,
　　And ſtill the fragrant Wounds are freſh.

Oh, Heart that, with a double Tide
　　Of BLOOD and Water maketh pure ;
O FLESH once offered on the Croſs,
　　The Gift that makes our pardon ſure ;
Let never more our ſinful Souls
　　The anguiſh of Thy Croſs renew ;
Nor forge again the cruel nails
　　That pierced Thy Victim BODY through.

𝔄 𝕳𝖞𝖒𝖓 𝖔𝖓 𝖙𝖍𝖊 𝕽𝖊𝖆𝖑 𝕻𝖗𝖊𝖘𝖊𝖓𝖈𝖊, 𝖔𝖋 𝖙𝖍𝖊 𝖝𝖎𝖛. 𝕮𝖊𝖓𝖙𝖚𝖗𝖞.

O Panis Dulciſſime.

BREAD of Life, Divinely ſweet,
　　Faithful Souls may take and eat,
　　　'Tis the Manna GOD hath ſent :
　　Gentle LAMB of GOD, in Thee
That great Sacrifice we ſee,
　　Which the Law and Prophets meant.
Though but common Bread appear,
Thy Dear FLESH is hidden here ;
　　On It now by faith we feed :
Holy SPIRIT, on us ſhine—
Seven-fold Gifts of Grace are Thine—
　　Make It now our Meat indeed.

Souls are quickened, bleſt, and fed,
When they eat this living Bread,
    Uncorruptedly the ſame ;
All their guilt is purified
By the FLESH of Him Who died—
    Glory to His precious Name.
Thus Thy ſacred Cup of BLOOD
And Thy FLESH, our myſtic Food,
    Cheer us while on earth we live :
But in Heaven to meet Thee, LORD,
There to feaſt around Thy Board,
    This will boundleſs Rapture give.

𝕿𝖍𝖊 𝕸𝖎𝖗𝖆𝖈𝖑𝖊𝖘 𝖔𝖋 𝕲𝖗𝖆𝖈𝖊 𝖆𝖓𝖉 𝕹𝖆𝖙𝖚𝖗𝖊.

This is the LORD's doing, and it is marvellous in our eyes.

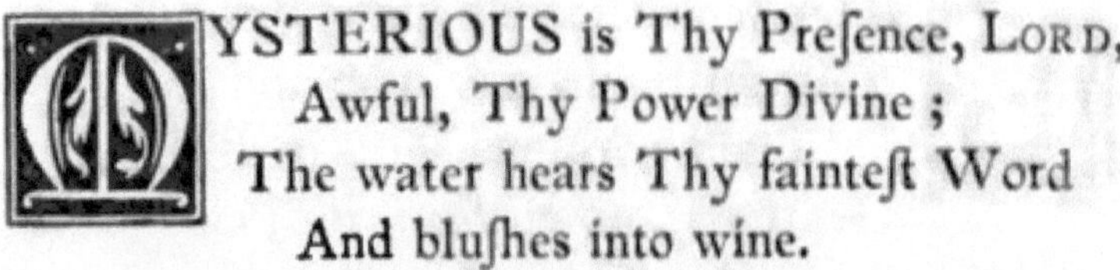

MYSTERIOUS is Thy Preſence, LORD,
    Awful, Thy Power Divine ;
The water hears Thy fainteſt Word
    And bluſhes into wine.

The clouds, that round us dark and low,
    With threatening aſpect move,
If Thou doſt look upon them, glow
    With rainbow lights of love.

The grain, that from the ſower's hand,
    Is ſcattered on the mould,

Soon in the valleys thick ſhall ſtand,
   Returned a thouſand fold.

The dews, which evening ſkies diſtil,
   Around the creeping vine,
At Thy Command ariſe and fill
   The blood-red grape with wine.

Thus holy Truths around us lie,
   Doing their humble part,
But wanting the attentive eye,
   And the believing heart.

Thus at Thy Holy Feaſt, O Lord,
   We kneel, and we believe
That That which Thy creative Word
   Hath made It, we receive.

Myſterious Truth, which human pride
   Muſt bow to and adore,
Which in our heart of hearts we hide,
   Believe, and aſk no more.

𝔄 𝔖equence of tɦe ꭗvi. 𝔠entury.

Ave! Caro Christi *Regis.*

HAIL! Flesh of Christ the Regal,
    Hail! Food that feeds the Flock,
The new Law's Heavenly Manna,
    The Spiritual Rock;

Can the blind world reject Thee ?
  Oh, Thou art All to us,
Adorable for ever,
  And wholly Marvellous.

With adoration hourly,
  With voices Heavenly ſweet,
The Faithful give Thee Glory
  As it is right and meet ;
And Thou wilt deign accept them—
  But would they feed on Thee
They muſt be pure and ſtainleſs,
  For Thou art Purity.

The Bride gives Thee her worſhip,
  Who art the Bread of Life ;
Thou Guide unto the pilgrim,
  Thou Peace where guilt is rife :
Salvation's Bread, oh, fill us
  With Thy unclouded Joy,
Sweet Food of Satisfaction,
  Pure Drink which cannot cloy.

Oh, be Thou nigh to guard us,
  The fallen one's Stay Thou art,
Balm to the weary mourner,
  Joy to the breaking heart ;
Thou didſt go firſt to light us,
  Thou haſt the path full trod ;
Guide through this world of grieving
  Into the Joy of God.

Corpus Christi.

Give the LORD *the honour due unto His Name ; worship
the* LORD *with holy worship.*

THESE Wounds I hail, O LORD my GOD,
    For they were suffered once for me ;
My ransom was Thy Precious BLOOD,
    My confidence is fixed in Thee.

Oh, Sacrifice beyond compare,
    High Priest and Victim both in One ;
All Love, all Light, all Wise, all Fair,
    The Virgin-Born, the FATHER'S SON.

Ten thousand thousand daily feed
    On Thee, and find their Graces grow ;
Sweet Help in every time of need,
    The Well, whence Heavenly Waters flow.

Lo ! how the broken-hearted come
    To see their SAVIOUR on the Cross ;
And then return in comfort home
    To count for Him all things but dross.

Sweet JESUS, stretch abroad Thine Arms,
    Embrace the world Thou hast redeemed ;
Thy Voice shall hush its loud alarms,
    And darkness fly where Thou hast beamed.

Thou, with Thy Saints, ſhalt reign alone
    From ſhore to ſhore, from pole to pole ;
And Glory round Thy holy Throne
    Shall in eternal ſurges roll.

And till the Trump of God may ſound,
    Thy Church on earth ſhall proſtrate fall,
In praiſe, and prayer, and hymns profound
    To worſhip Thee, the Lord of All.

The Love of Chriſt for His Spouſe.

*He brought me to the Banqueting houſe, and His Banner
over me was Love.*

ESU, we thus obey
    Thy laſt and kindeſt Word,
And in Thine own appointed way
    We come to meet Thee, Lord.

Thus we remember Thee,
    And take this Bread and Wine,
As Thine own dying Legacy,
    And our Redemption's Sign.

Thy Preſence makes the Feaſt ;
    Now let our Spirits feel
The Glory not to be expreſt,
    The Joy unſpeakable.

With high and Heavenly Blifs
Thou doft our Spirit cheer ;
Thy Houfe of banqueting is this,
And Thou haft brought us here.

Now let our Souls be fed
With Manna from above,
And over us Thy Banner fpread
Of everlafting Love.

A Prose, of the xv. Century.

Ave ! Verum Corpus *natum.*

HAIL to Thee, True Body ! Sprung
From the Virgin Mary's Womb,
The Same that on the Crofs was hung,
And bore for man the bitter doom :
Hear us, Merciful and Mild,
Jesu, Mary's Gracious Child.

From Whofe Side, for finners riven,
Water flowed and mingled Blood ;
MayftThou, Deareft Lord, be given,
In death's hour to be my Food :
Hear us, Merciful and Mild,
Jesu, Mary's Gracious Child.

Prayer for the Fulfilment of a Promise.

*I will commune with thee from above the
Mercy-ſeat.*

LORD, when before Thy Throne we meet,
　　Thy Goodneſs to adore,
　　From Heaven th' eternal Mercy-ſeat
　　On us Thy Bleſſing pour,
And make our inmoſt Souls to be
An habitation meet for Thee.

The BODY for our Ranſom given ;
　　The BLOOD in Mercy ſhed ;
With this immortal Food from Heaven,
　　LORD, let our Souls be fed ;
And as we round Thy Table kneel,
Help us Thy quickening Grace to feel.

Be Thou, O HOLY SPIRIT, nigh,
　　Accept the humble prayer,
The contrite Soul's repentant ſigh,
　　The ſinner's heartfelt tear ;
And let our adoration riſe,
As fragrant incenſe, to the ſkies.

A Penitential Hymn ; after long neglect of the Blessed Sacrament.

I am no more worthy to be called Thy Son.

UR Lord in Words of Heavenly Wis-
dom said—
We must not cast to dogs the Children's
Bread ;
Yet even dogs, within their master's hall,
May eat the crumbs that from his table fall.
My FATHER, here a Child unworthy comes,
Beneath Thy Board to gather up the Crumbs ;
No longer worthy to be called Thy Child,
So far has sin my wayward heart beguiled.

Thy Grace preventing called me by my name,
When yet unconscious to the font I came ;
Made Child of God by free Adoption there,
And taught to call Thee FATHER in my prayer.
Yet have I followed worldly ways and vain,
And empty husks are all that now remain ;
On joys unreal have I my substance spent,
My feet are bare, my garments soiled and rent.

Now, taking with me words, I'll straight arise,
And seek my FATHER in this woful guise ;
For well I know a parent's bowels yearn,
Whene'er he sees a long-lost child return.

Before affliction came I went aſtray ;
But now, am bent to keep Thy righteous Way :
Lo ! while I yet am ſpeaking He doth hear ;
Yea, e'en before I called, He haſtened near :

He brings forth that beſt robe to put me on,
The Righteous Robe of His Begotten Son ;
And bids my feet, which ſlippery paths have trod,
With Goſpel Peace henceforth be firmly ſhod.
If Angels joy when ſinners leave their way,
Thoſe elder Brothers will rejoice to-day,
That I, with purpoſe fixed new life to lead,
Now come repentant at Thy Board to feed.

By faith I ſee CHRIST's BODY in This Bread,
And in this Cup His BLOOD for ſinners ſhed ;
Which, though my mind tries vainly to conceive,
As CHRIST hath ſpoken, ſo do I believe.
No longer now ſelf-baniſhed from my place,
'Mongſt thoſe who, ever with Thee, ſhare Thy
　　　Grace,
On Heavenly Manna ſhall my Soul be fed :
LORD, give me evermore Thy Children's Bread.

Let me not only in Thy Houſehold dwell,
For ſervants hired know not their maſter well ;
With CHRIST ſo cloſe let my Communion be,
That I may dwell in Him, and He in me.
Then, with the Angel-choir, my voice I'll raiſe,
More bound than they redeeming Love to praiſe :
Not one has erred of all that Heavenly Hoſt ;
Thoſe who have moſt forgiven, will love Thee moſt.

Hymn to Jesus in the Blessed Sacrament.

*Behold, O God our Defender, and look upon the Face
of Thine Anointed.*

JESUS, True God, True Man we adore
  Thee ;
  Veiled though Thy Presence, we hail
  Thee here ;
True Bread of Angels, we worship before Thee,
 Now the blest moment has brought Thee so near.

Thou dost descend, but no awful thunder
 Rending the Heavens o'erwhelms us with dread ;
Silently, filling our Spirits with wonder,
 Thou dost stoop down to us, Life-giving Bread.

Vision of Peace and Fountain of Pity,
 Praise of the Angels, and Perfect Love,
Thou art the Gate of the Heavenly City,
 Glory of Saints in the mansions above.

Now, at Thy Shrine, Thou liest before us,
 Thou, Who for sinners sought Mary's Breast ;
Sweetly is ringing the Angels' glad chorus,
 Bethlehem, true House of Bread, is our rest.

Here Precious Blood for sin is still flowing,
 Sealing forgiveness and making us pure ;
Thou in the Gift of Thyself art bestowing,
 Grace to endeavour, and Strength to endure.

Now may we cry, while kneeling before Thee,
　　Lifting our hearts to the FATHER's dread
　　　　Throne—
Look on the Face of Thy CHRIST, we implore
　　　　Thee,
　　Spare our tranſgreſſions, our Sacrifice own.

JESUS, all hail! Redeemer moſt holy,
　　Thee we adore at Thine Altar-ſhrine ;
Keep evermore our hearts pure and lowly,
　　Meet for Thy Preſence, O Victim Divine.

A Hymn of Santolius of S. Victor, of the xvii. Century.

The BLOOD *of* JESUS CHRIST *cleanſeth us from all ſin.*

O CHRIST, Who art enthroned on high,
　　Look on us, parted far from Thee ;
How wondrouſly Thou comeſt nigh,
　　That joinèd with us Thou mayſt be,
By that ſame BODY, Which, at birth
Shed joy and gladneſs over earth.

Hence, like a mountain torrent's flow,
　　Grace downward pours in copious ſtreams,
Oh, when that fervent Love doth glow,
　　What heart but melts beneath its beams ?
　　What guilty Soul would ſhun the Flood,
　　And not ſeek cleanſing in that BLOOD ?

O haughty man, lay down thy pride,
 Thy LORD is here in Meekneſs found ;
Why ſtrayeſt thou, when He doth hide
 Himſelf within this narrow bound ?
  Why wilt thou ſeek the gazing crowd,
  When GOD is veiled beneath a Cloud ?

All Glory to the FATHER be,
 Who in His Might the world did frame ;
And to the SON, Who ſet us free
 By dying on the Croſs in ſhame ;
  And unto Him, Whoſe quickening Breath
  Doth raiſe us up anew from death.

A Hymn of Angelus to the Good Shepherd, of the xvii. Century.

Guter Hirte, willſt du nicht.

WILT Thou not, my Shepherd true,
  Spare Thy ſheep, in Mercy ſpare
   me ?
 Wilt Thou not, as ſhepherds do,
 In Thine Arms rejoicing bear me ;
Bear me where all troubles ceaſe,
Home to Folds of Joy and Peace ?

 See how I have gone aſtray,
  How earth's labyrinths oft miſlead me ;

Bring me back into the way,
   In Thine own green Paſtures feed me :
Gather me within the Fold,
Where Thy lambs Thy Light behold.

With Thy Flock I long to be,
   With the Flock to whom 'tis given
Safe to feed, and, praiſing Thee,
   Roam the happy plains of Heaven :
Free from fear of ſinful ſtain,
They can never ſtray again.

Lord, I here am ſore beſet,
   Fears at every ſtep confound me ;
Lo ! my foes have ſpread their net,
   And with craft and might ſurround me :
Such their ſnares on every ſide,
Safe Thy ſheep can ne'er abide.

Jesus, Lord, my Shepherd true,
   Oh, from wolves Thy ſheep deliver ;
Help, as ſhepherds wont to do,
   From their jaws preſerve me ever :
Bid Thy trembling wanderer come
To his everlaſting Home.

The Origin of the Church.

En, ut superba criminum.

 O ! how the ſavage crew
Of our proud ſins hath rent
The Heart of our All-gracious GOD—
That Heart ſo Innocent.

The ſoldier's quiv'ring lance,
Our guilt it was that ſped;
The ſteel that pierced Him, by our crimes
So deadly ſharp was made.

O Heart, whence ſprang the Church,
The SAVIOUR's ſpotleſs Bride,
Thou Door of our Salvation's Ark
Set in its myſtic Side,

Thou holy Fount, whence flows
The ſacred ſevenfold Flood,
Where we our filthy robes may cleanſe
In the LAMB's Saving BLOOD,

By ſorrowful relapſe,
Thee will we rend no more;
But like the flames, thoſe types of Love,
Strive Heavenward to ſoar.

FATHER and SON Supreme,
And SPIRIT, hear our cry;
To Whom Praiſe, Power, and Glory be
Through all Eternity.

The earthly Prieſthood Divine.

O Sacerdotum veneranda jura.

AWFUL is the Prieſtly ſtate,
    Which, by faith beheld aright,
Cloſes and unbars the gate,
    Though unſeen by mortal ſight:
CHRIST, in this His earthly Seat,
Holds in them the Balance meet,
Binds and lets the ſinner's feet
    In His own appointed Rite.

When they ply their healing art,
    'Tis His Hand in them is found;
When they ſoothe the wounded heart,
    His Anointing heals the wound:
When they ſpeak, the faithful ſheep
Drink their words and hide them deep,
For the Law of GOD they ſteep
    Firſt in their own hearts profound.

When the Wrath is going forth,
    And the Vial in mid air,

They ſtand forth to ſtop the Wrath
  With deep importuning prayer :
May they, LORD, themſelves be wiſe,
Who touch Thy dread Myſteries,
Mirrors, in their people's eyes,
  Worthy of the things they bear.

FATHER, SPIRIT, SON DIVINE,
  Who doſt reſcue from the grave,
From Heaven's central echoing ſhrine
  Let Thy Glory, wave on wave,
Fill the all-ſurrounding ſea
Of ſhoreleſs Eternity,
Singing, Prieſt of Prieſts, of Thee,
  And Thy mighty Power to ſave.

𝕿𝖍𝖊 𝖂𝖊𝖉𝖉𝖎𝖓𝖌 𝕲𝖆𝖗𝖒𝖊𝖓𝖙.

*Dum Veſtem audis Nuptialem, ne de veſtimentis, quibus
induimur, id exiſtimes, ſed de bonis operibus.*

THE nuptial Robe, which all muſt wear
      Who enter to the Spouſal Feaſt,
    Is not a garb for vulgar ſtare,
      A cloth of gold, in ſamite pieced,
In coſtly jewels glittering fair,
With ruſtling pride ſurceaſed.

The nuptial Robe which all muſt don,
   Who would their heads lift up on high,
Who would approach the Bridal Throne
   With contrite heart and ſuppliant eye,
This yoke of Peace, and this alone,
   Is the fair ſtole of Charity.

The nuptial Robe is pure and white,
   Unſoiled in deed, unſtained in thought,
With willing heart and purpoſe right,
   In works of Love it muſt be wrought,
Although 'tis wove with colours bright,
   It ſhall not paſs where Love is not.

The nuptial Robe, to which is given
   An entrance to the Bliſs of GOD,
Muſt raiſe the Soul with Virtue's leaven,
   Muſt to the Croſs point out the road,
And humbly labour ſtill, till Heaven
   Relieve thee of thy heavy load.

Then, clothed anew in Virtue's dreſs,
   Angels ſhall bid thee welcome home ;
Then ſhall the toil that did oppreſs
   Be buried with thee in the tomb ;
Then ſhall ye hear that laſt addreſs—
   Ye bleſſed of My FATHER, come.

The Rose of Sharon; a German Hymn of the xv. Century.

I am the Roſe of Sharon.

KNOW a Flower ſo ſweet and fair,
    There is no earthly bloſſom
With Sharon's Roſe that may compare;
    Fain would I wear
Its Fragrance in my boſom.

It is the True and Living WORD,
    Whom GOD Himſelf hath given
To be our Guide, our Light, our LORD,
    In Whom is ſtored
All hope for earth and Heaven.

Hark, how He ſaith—Come unto Me
    Ye burdened and ſad-hearted;
Granted your heart's deſire ſhall be,
    And pardon free,
To mourning Souls imparted.

This is My BODY that I give,
    For you in Mercy broken;
Whate'er is Mine with It receive,
    If ye believe
And keep what I have ſpoken.

This is My Blood, once ſhed for you,
   Ye hearts, now faint and ſinking;
Drink of My Cup, and find anew
   Freſh Strength to do
My Bidding without ſhrinking.

Ah, Lord, by Thy moſt bitter Woes
   We pray Thee, ne'er forſake us;
Since Thou couldſt even die for thoſe
   Who were Thy foes,
Thy Children deign to make us.

And keep us ever cloſe to Thee,
   Give courage to confeſs Thee,
However dark the time may be,
   Till ſafe and free
In Heaven at laſt we bleſs Thee.

The Bread that cometh down from Heaven.

They need not depart; give ye them to eat.

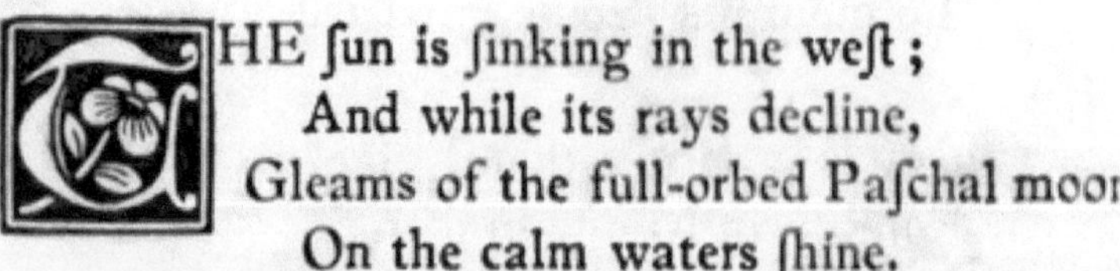

THE ſun is ſinking in the weſt;
   And while its rays decline,
Gleams of the full-orbed Paſchal moon
   On the calm waters ſhine.

The Galilean waters huſhed
   In eventide are ſtill;

Yet crowds of weary wanderers wait
  Upon its lonely hill.

Pilgrims they are, for Sion bound,
  Whose Paschal Feast is near;
But the true Passover Himself
  Receives and feeds them here.

They sit upon the grassy turf
  Marshalled in groups and rows;
Christ holds the food, which in His Hand,
  And by His Blessing grows.

He gives the food; Apostles take,
  Distribute it, and then—
Two fishes and five barley loaves
  Regale five thousand men.

O Blessed Lord, the earth is Thine,
  By Thy creative Hand
The golden harvests crown the year
  And deck the fertile land.

O Blessed Lord, Thou Bread of Life,
  That cometh down from Heaven,
Supplies of everlasting Good
  By Thee to man are given.

Thy Godhead is the Well-spring, Lord,
  The pure exhaustless Source,

From which they flow through age to age,
In never-ending courſe.

In channels formed by Thee, they flow
In rivulets of Grace,
Refreſhing all who wander here
In this world's deſert place.

Oh, feed us, weary pilgrims, LORD,
And to Thy Sion bring,
To keep a Heavenly Feaſt with Thee,
Our Prophet, Prieſt, and King.

PART V.

THE THANKSGIVING.

The Canticle of S. Teresa after Holy Communion.

Vivo sin vivir en mi.

THIS Union of Divineſt Love,
By which I live a Life above,
Setting my heart at liberty,
My GOD to me enchains;
But then to ſee His Majeſty
In ſuch a baſe captivity,
It ſo my Spirit pains,
That evermore I weep and ſigh,
Dying, becauſe I do not die.

Ah, what a length does life appear;
How hard to bear this exile here;
How hard from weary day to day
To pine without relief:

The yearning hope to break away
From this my priſon-houſe of clay,
  Inſpires ſo ſharp a grief,
That overcome I weep and ſigh,
Dying, becauſe I do not die.

Oh, what a bitter life is this,
Deprived of GOD, its only Bliſs;
  And what though Love delicious be,
    Not ſo is Hope deferred:
  Ah, then, Dear LORD, in Charity,
  This iron weight of miſery
    From my poor Soul ungird;
For evermore I weep and ſigh,
Dying, becauſe I do not die.

This only gives me life and ſtrength,
To know that die I muſt at length;
  For Hope inſures me Bliſs Divine,
    Through death, and death alone.
  O Death, for thee, for thee I pine,
  Sweet Death, of Life the origin,
    Ah, wing thee hither ſoon;
For evermore I weep and ſigh,
Dying, becauſe I do not die.

And thou, fond Life, oh, vex me not,
By ſtill prolonging here my lot,
  But know that Love is urging me;
  Know that the only way

To gain thee, is—by losing thee.
Come then, O Death, come speedily,
  And end thy long delay;
For evermore I weep and sigh,
Dying, because I do not die.

The Life above, the Life on high,
Alone is Life in verity;
  Nor can we Life at all enjoy,
    Till this poor life is o'er;
  Then, O sweet Death, no longer fly
  From me, who, ere my time to die,
    Am dying evermore;
For evermore I weep and sigh,
Dying, because I do not die.

To Him Who deigns in me to live,
What better Gift have I to give,
  O my poor earthly life, than thee?
    Too glad of thy decay,
  So but I may the sooner see
  That Face of sweetest Majesty,
    For which I pine away;
While evermore I weep and sigh,
Dying, because I do not die.

  Absent from Thee, my SAVIOUR Dear,
I call not Life this living here;
  But a long dying agony,
    The sharpest I have known;

And I myſelf, myſelf to ſee
In ſuch a rack of miſery,
  For very pity moan ;
And ever, ever weep and ſigh,
Dying, becauſe I do not die.

The fiſh that from the brook is ta'en,
Soon finds an end of all its pain ;
  And agonies the worſt to bear
    Are ſooneſt ſpent and o'er ;
  But what acuteſt death can e'er
  With this my painful life compare
    In torture evermore ?
While evermore I weep and ſigh,
Dying, becauſe I do not die.

When on the Altar I eſpy,
My GOD, Thy hidden Majeſty,
  And peace is ſoothing my ſad heart,
    Then comes redoubled pain,
  To think, that here from Thee apart,
  I cannot ſee Thee as Thou art ;
    But gaze and gaze in vain ;
While evermore I weep and ſigh,
Dying, becauſe I do not die.

When with the hope I comfort me,
At leaſt in Heaven of ſeeing Thee,
  The thought that I may loſe Thee yet,
    With anguiſh thrills me through ;

And by a thousand fears beset,
My very hope inspires regret,
    And multiplies my woe ;
While evermore I weep and sigh,
Dying, because I do not die.

Ah, Lord, my Light and living Breath,
Take me, oh, take me from this death,
    And burst the bars that sever me
        From my true Life above ;
    Think how I die Thy Face to see,
    And cannot live away from Thee,
        O my eternal Love :
And ever, ever weep and sigh,
Dying, because I do not die.

I weary of this endless strife ;
I weary of this dying life ;
    This living death, this heavy chain,
        This torment of delay,
    In which her sins my Soul detain ;
    Ah, when shall it be mine ? Ah, when,
        With my last breath to say—
No more I weep, no more I sigh ;
I'm dying of desire to die ?

Sacramental Union with Christ.

I will love him, and will manifest Myself to him.

WHAT happiness can equal mine?
    I've found the Object of my love;
My Saviour and my Lord Divine
    Is come to me from Heaven above:
He makes my heart His own Abode;
    His Flesh becomes my daily Bread;
He pours on me His Healing Blood;
    And with His Life my Soul is fed.

My Love is mine, and I am His;
    In me He dwells, in Him I live:
Where could I taſte a purer Bliſs?
    What greater Boon could Jesus give?
O Royal Banquet, Heavenly Feaſt,
    O flowing Fount of Life and Grace,
Where God the Giver, man the gueſt,
    Meet and unite in ſweet embrace.

Dear Jesus, now my heart is Thine,
    Oh, may it never from Thee fly;
My God, be Thou for ever mine,
    And I, Thine own eternally.
No more, O Satan, thee I fear,
    O World, thy charms I now deſpiſe;
For Christ Himſelf is with me here,
    My Joy, my Life, my Paradiſe.

The Crown of Victory.

Steil und dornig ift der Pfad.

STEEP and thorny is the way,
　　Straight to Heaven our home af-
　　　　cending;
　　Happy he who every day
Walks therein, for CHRIST contending;
　　　　Happy when, his journey o'er,
　　　　Conqueror he to CHRIST fhall foar.

Great fhall be his recompenfe,
　　True to death on GOD who waited;
Who renounced the joys of fenfe,
　　To his SAVIOUR confecrated;
　　　　Who has gazed with fteadfaft eye
　　　　On the Crown of Victory.

On the Crofs our Dying LORD
　　Bled for man who had offended,
Purchafed us the great Reward,
　　Then from earth to Heaven afcended:
　　　　Victory e'en in death, He faid—
　　　　FATHER, it is finifhèd.

May we foon approach Thee near,
　　We who long on earth have ftriven,
Storms and night furround us here,
　　Bright and peaceful 'tis in Heaven:

Death may ſtrike, and graves may yawn,
Yonder beams Life's endleſs dawn.

On then, comrades, wend your way,
    Let not life's drear waſte alarm you ;
Look to JESUS, watch and pray
    'Gainſt the fight that GOD would arm you.
      GOD, Who ſtrong the weak canſt make,
      Victory give for JESU's ſake.

In hac Cruce Te invenit, quicunque invenit.

Circumire poſſum cœlum et terram, mare et aridum, et nuſquam Te inveniam, niſi in Cruce.

HAIL ! Tree of Life, planted anew,
    Amidſt the briar-waſte of dearth,
    Once more thy branches dropping dew
    Awake the echoes deep of mirth,
Loſt ſince the airs of Eden blew
    Their ſweet laſt gift o'er ſin-ſtained earth.

Hail ! Tree of Life, on Calvary's height
    Extending wide, reſtored again ;
Hail ! happy boughs of ſweet delight,
    Where ſure repoſe and quiet reign ;
A ſhelter they from demon ſpite,
    From ſorrowing care, and fruitleſs pain.

Hail! Tree of Life, beneath thy ſhade
   Fain would I reſt, and liſt thy call ;
No burning heat ſhall ſtrike my head,
   No mildew there, nor blight ſhall fall ;
For, ſhould the bitter cup invade,
   Sweet Peace is there to temper all.

Hail! ſaving Croſs, beneath thy foot,
   Here would I reſt, and look above ;
My needed ſtrength would here recruit,
   Thy promiſed Mercies here would prove,
Gather each day increaſe of fruit,
   New fuel for increaſe of Love.

𝕿𝖍𝖊 𝕷𝖆𝖘𝖙 𝕮𝖔𝖒𝖒𝖚𝖓𝖎𝖔𝖓 𝖎𝖓 𝕮𝖍𝖚𝖗𝖈𝖍.

LORD, *now letteſt Thou Thy ſervant depart in peace.*

HE hath been near unto the golden Gate :
   Serene he waited for his Maſter's
      Calling :
   It came—A little longer thou muſt wait,
The ſands of life have not yet ceaſed their falling.

Once more he paſſeth in the well-known way ;
   Though ſight be dim, and footſteps fail and
      falter,
Led by the hand, once more this Holy Day
   He draweth nigh unto his LORD's dear Altar.

He kneeleth low; he heareth words of Bliſs;
   With hand up-ſpread and eyelid cloſed he
      kneeleth.
Oh, what an hour of peace and joy is this:
   Oh, in what Love his LORD Himſelf revealeth.

We ſee the trembling form: but far from ſight
   The Spirit paſſeth to more glorious regions,
Behind the veil, upborne on wings of light,
   Blending its worſhip with Angelic legions.

Entranced he gazeth on the wounded Side,
   The precious Stream for him in Mercy flowing,
The low-bowed Head, the Arms outſtretching wide,
   The awful Croſs with myſtic radiance glowing.

Servant of GOD, thou haſt not long to ſtay;
   Soon the weak bonds that hold thee here ſhall
      ſever;
Then ſhalt thou gaze upon the perfeƈt day,
   And be with Him thou lov'ſt for ever and for ever.

The Wounded Side.

Dignare me, O JESU, *rogo Te.*

JESU, grant me this, I pray,
   Ever in Thy Heart to ſtay;
Let me evermore abide
   Hidden in Thy wounded Side.

If the evil one prepare,
Or the world, a tempting ſnare,
I am ſafe when I abide
In Thy Heart and wounded Side.

If the fleſh, more dangerous ſtill,
Tempt my Soul to deeds of ill,
Nought I fear when I abide
In Thy Heart and wounded Side.

Death will come one day to me ;
Jesu, caſt me not from Thee :
Dying, let me ſtill abide
In Thy Heart and wounded Side.

Self-dedication to God: a Hymn of Angelus, of the xvii. Century.

Nun nimm mein Herz und alles was ich bin.

NOW take my heart, and all that is in me,
My Lord Beloved, take it from me to
Thee ;
I would have Thine :
This Soul and fleſh of mine
Would order thought and word and deed
As Thy moſt holy Will ſhall lead.

Thou feedeſt me with Heavenly Bread and Wine,
Thou poureſt through me ſtreams of Life Divine ;

O noble Face,
So Sweet, so full of Grace,
I ponder, as Thy Cross I see,
How best to give myself to Thee.

Behold, through all the eternal Ages, still
My heart shall choose and love Thy holy Will;
Wouldst Thou my death?
I die to Thee in faith;
Wouldst Thou that I should longer live?
To Thee the choice I wholly give.

But Thou must also deign to be my own,
To dwell in me, to make my heart Thy Throne,
My God indeed,
My Help in time of need,
My Head, from Whom no power can sever,
The Bridegroom of my Soul for ever.

Powerful to Save.

The Lord *grant unto him, that he may find Mercy
of the* Lord *in that Day.*

ON whose Soul have Mercy, Jesu, powerful to save—
This inscribe above my clay, when sleep-
ing in the grave:
The Cross o'ershadowing the spot; a tablet at the
feet,
Recording my baptismal name dear lips have rendered sweet.

For Mercy is my only hope, for Mercy is my cry,
I have no other plea to gain a bleſt Eternity;
I have no truſt but in the Croſs to ſave in my death-
      hour,
No help but in my SAVIOUR's BLOOD, to quench
      the tempter's power.

The ſolemn hour of cloſing life to all is drawing
      near,
When nothing but the COMFORTER can ſuccour
      or can cheer;
O Glorious TRIUNE, Light of Life, to Thee be
      Glory given,
For JESU Preſent when on earth, for JESU when
      in Heaven.

The New Ark.

Cor Arca Legem continens.

ARK of the Covenant, not that
    Whence bondage came of old,
But that of Pardon and of Grace
    And Mercies manifold,
Thou Veil of awful Myſtery,
    Thou Sanctuary ſublime,
Thou ſacred Temple, holier far
    Than that of olden time,

Bleſt Heart of CHRIST, in Thy dear Wound
    The hidden depth we ſee

Of what were elſe ungueſſed by us,
   His boundleſs Charity.
Beneath this emblem of pure Love
   'Twas Love Himſelf that died,
And offered up for us to God
   A Victim crucified.

Oh, who of His redeemed will Him
   Their mutual Love refuſe?
Who would not rather in that Heart
   Their Home eternal chooſe?
To God the FATHER, God the SON,
   And HOLY GHOST, to Thee
Be Honour, Glory, Virtue, Power,
   Through all Eternity.

The Croſs of Chriſt.

O Crux, qui ſola languentes.

CROSS, that only know'ſt the Woes
   He ſuffered erſt Who hung on Thee,
Speak to our hearts of thoſe deep Throes,
   Thoſe broken Words, that Agony.

Sharp were the nails which ruthleſs bound
   His fainting Form in thine embrace;
The thorns about His Temples wound,
   Forbade Him e'en that reſting-place.

Oh, fearful Woe—the LORD of Life
  Upon thy breaſt contends with death ;
And, Victor in the mortal ſtrife,
  Yet yielded up His laſt faint Breath.

O holy Croſs, by thee we live ;
  And at thy foot our life we lay :
Tribunal, whence our LORD ſhall give
  His Judgment, in that bitter Day.

Give us, O LORD, to die with Thee,
  With Thee, fell Death to riſe above,
Deſpiſing earthly vanity,
  To fix our hearts on Joys above.

The FATHER praiſe we ; and the SON
  Who triumphed for us on the Tree,
And hath for us that Glory won ;
  Like praiſe unto the SPIRIT be.

𝕸emento 𝕮hristi.

Halt im Gedächtniſs JESUM CHRIST.

BEAR JESUS CHRIST the LORD in mind,
  Who left His Heavenly Throne,
And, out of Love to humankind,
  Put human nature on—
Our Brother, born of Fleſh and Blood,
To make His ſure Salvation good ;
  Then thank Him for His Love.

Bear Jesus Christ the Lord in mind,
On Whom our hopes depend,
With that great Love He bore mankind
He loved them to the end ;
And gave at length His Flesh and Blood
To be their Souls' ſuſtaining Food ;
Then thank Him for His Love.

Bear Jesus Christ the Lord in mind,
Who ſore by grief was tried ;
Out of pure Love to humankind
Upon the Croſs He died :
He vanquiſhed ſin and every foe,
And ſaved us from eternal woe ;
Then thank Him for His Love.

Bear Jesus Christ the Lord in mind,
Who, freed from death and pain,
In His great Love to humankind,
The third day roſe again ;
The Righteouſneſs of Christ the Lord
Has Life and Peace to man reſtored ;
Then thank Him for His Love.

Bear Jesus Christ the Lord in mind,
Who, having drained His Cup,
In His great Love to humankind
To Heaven aſcended up ;
There to prepare for us a Place,
Where we ſhall always ſee His Face,
And thank Him for His Love.

Bear JESUS CHRIST the LORD in mind,
  Once more from Heaven above
He'll come, as Judge of humankind,
  The quick and dead to prove:
Take heed that thou mayſt ſtand the teſt,
And enter then His holy Reſt,
    To thank Him for His Love.

LORD, let me ever bear in mind,
  And with true faith embrace
Thy Love to me and all mankind,
  And may Thy cheering Grace
In hours of ſorrow comfort give,
And cauſe me after death to live,
    And thank Thee for Thy Love.

𝕿𝖍𝖊 𝕾𝖍𝖎𝖕 𝖎𝖓 𝖙𝖍𝖊 𝖒𝖎𝖉𝖘𝖙 𝖔𝖋 𝖙𝖍𝖊 𝕾𝖊𝖆.

And JESUS *went unto them, walking on the ſea.*

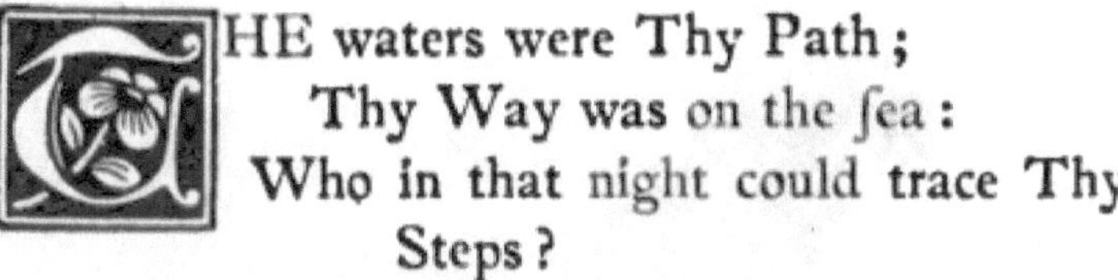

THE waters were Thy Path;
  Thy Way was on the ſea:
Who in that night could trace Thy
    Steps?
Who ſolve the Myſtery?

Some at Capernaum aſked—
  When and how cam'ſt Thou here?
In vain they tried to find the track
  By which Thou didſt appear.

But Thy Diſciples, LORD,
 Did gladly Thee receive;
And when the ſhip was at the ſhore;
 They pry not, but believe.

LORD, in Thy Sacraments
 Thou walkeſt on the ſea;
Let us not aſk—how doſt Thou come?
 But gladly welcome Thee.

Then will the winds be huſhed,
 The waves no longer roar;
When CHRIST is with us in the Ship,
 The Ship is at the ſhore.

Give to the FATHER praiſe,
 And praiſe be to the SON,
Praiſe be to the HOLY GHOST,
 Praiſe to the THREE in ONE.

A Hymn of S. Bernard.

JESU, *Dulcedo cordium.*

JESUS, Thou Joy of loving hearts,
 Thou Fount of Life, Thou Light of
  men,
 From the beſt bliſs that earth imparts,
We turn unfilled to Thee again.

Thy Truth unchanged hath ever ſtood ;
  Thou ſaveſt thoſe that on Thee call ;
To them that ſeek Thee, Thou art Good ;
  To them that find Thee, All in All.

We taſte Thee, O Thou living Bread,
  And long to feaſt upon Thee ſtill ;
We drink of Thee, the fountain Head,
  And thirſt our Souls from Thee to fill.

Our reſtleſs Spirits yearn for Thee,
  Where'er our changeful lot is caſt ;
Glad, when Thy gracious Smile we ſee,
  Bleſt, when our faith can hold Thee faſt.

O Jesus, ever with us ſtay ;
  Make all our moments calm and bright ;
Chaſe the dark night of ſin away ;
  Shed o'er the world Thy holy Light.

Communion Calm and Joy.

Peace I leave with you ; My Peace I give unto you.

H, what is this enchanting Calm,
    Which thus with Joy my boſom fills,
  Which o'er my Spirit pours a balm,
    And through my inmoſt being thrills ?

Is ſome bright Seraph higher ſent,
  Diffuſing ſweetneſs from his wings,
To ſteep my boſom in content,
  Unſeen, unfelt from earthly things?

No; ſomething purer far muſt dwell
  Within this raptured Soul of mine :
'Tis what no mortal tongue can tell ;
  'Tis more than Heavenly, 'tis Divine.

My God, my Jesus, it is Thou
  Art raviſhing my heart with Bliſs ;
Thy Preſence is within me now :
  Could I have aſked a boon like this?

Yes, ſtooping from Thy Throne above,
  Thou wilt not dwell from man apart :
Thou, in Thy Sacrament of Love,
  Haſt come to dwell within my heart.

𝕮𝖍𝖊 𝕷𝖆ſ𝖙 𝕾𝖆𝖈𝖗𝖆𝖒𝖊𝖓𝖙𝖘.

Yea, though I walk through the Valley of the Shadow
of Death, I will fear no evil ; for Thou art with me,
Thy Rod and Thy Staff comfort me.

HEN day's ſhadows lengthen,
  Jesu, be Thou near ;
Pardon, comfort, ſtrengthen,
  Chaſe away my fear ;

Love and Hope be deepened,
  Faith more ſtrong and clear.

When the night grows darkeſt,
  And the ſtars are pale,
When the foe aſſembles
  In Death's miſty vale,
Be Thou Sword and Helmet,
  Be Thou Shield and Mail.

He, who ſtands beſide me,
  Comes but to proclaim
Pardon for contrition,
  Wipes out ſtains of ſhame,
Saying—I abſolve thee
  In CHRIST's bleſſed Name.

If Thou willeſt, feed me,
  Strengthen, ere I go ;
In that unknown pathway
  Lighten every woe ;
JESU, as Thou knoweſt,
  Grant me ſo to know.

That an hour of weakness—
  That a time of fear—
Come, Thou Bread of Heaven,
  Sacrament ſo dear ;
All I loved may vaniſh
  If but Thou be near.

Come, Thou Food of Angels,
   Source of every Grace,
In Thy FATHER's Manſions
   Give me ſoon a place,
That unveiled in Splendour
   I may ſee Thy Face.

Fading this world, fading,
   Forms are growing dim,
Other voices whiſper
   Tones of ſome ſweet hymn,
Telling of His Mercy,
   Speaking but of Him.

By the Jordan's ripples,
   Paſſing through the ſhade ;
Let me hear that promiſe
   Once for ever made—
It is I, Thy JESUS ;
   Be not thou afraid.

Cold the waters rolling,
   Chill the miſts around,
Black the night above me,
   Strange th' untrodden ground,
Oft loſt in the deſert,
   Yet may I be found.

Then be near me, JESUS,
   Enemies ſhall flee ;

Ave! Sacramentum,
  Thou my Comfort be,
Food, and Prieſt, and Victim,
  Let me feed on Thee.

So ſhall no fears chill me
  On that unknown ſhore,
For in death He conquered
  And can die no more;
His Hand guards and guides me
  To the City's door.

Bleſſed warfare over,
  Endleſs Reſt alone,
Tears no more, nor ſorrow,
  Neither ſigh nor moan,
But a ſong of triumph
  Round about the Throne.

An Act of Thankſgiving after Reception.

Abide with us; for it is towards evening.

ESUS, Gentleſt Saviour,
  God of Might and Power,
Thou Thyſelf art dwelling
  In us at this hour.

Nature cannot hold Thee,
  Heaven is all too ſtrait

For Thine endleſs Glory,
    And Thy Royal State.

Out beyond the ſhining
    Of the fartheſt ſtar,
Thou art ever ſtretching
    Infinitely far.

Yet the hearts of children
    Hold what worlds can not,
And the GOD of Wonders
    Loves the lowly ſpot.

As men to their gardens
    Go to ſeek ſweet flowers,
In our hearts Dear JESUS
    Seeks them at all hours.

JESUS, Gentleſt SAVIOUR,
    Thou art in us now;
Fill us full of Goodneſs,
    Till our hearts o'erflow.

Pray the prayer within us
    That to Heaven ſhall riſe;
Sing the ſong that Angels
    Sing above the ſkies.

Multiply our Graces,
    Chiefly love and fear,

And, Dear LORD, the chiefeſt,
    Grace to perſevere.

Oh, how can we thank Thee
    For a Gift like this,
Gift that truly maketh
    Heaven's eternal Bliſs?

Ah, when wilt Thou always
    Make our hearts Thy home?
We muſt wait for Heaven,
    Then the day will come.

Now at leaſt we'll keep Thee
    All the time we may;
But Thy Grace and Bleſſing
    We will keep alway.

𝕿𝖍𝖆𝖓𝖐𝖘𝖌𝖎𝖛𝖎𝖓𝖌 𝖆𝖋𝖙𝖊𝖗 𝕮𝖔𝖒𝖒𝖚𝖓𝖎𝖔𝖓.

*Every day will I give thanks unto Thee, and praiſe Thy
Name for ever and ever.*

GOD of Mercy, GOD of Might,
How ſhould pale ſinners bear the ſight,
If, as Thy Power is ſurely here,
Thine open Glory ſhould appear?

For now Thy People are allowed
To ſcale the mount and pierce the cloud,
And Faith may feed her eager view
With wonders Sinai never knew.

Fresh from th' atoning Sacrifice
The world's Creator bleeding lies,
That man, His foe, by whom He bled,
May take Him for his daily Bread.

Oh, agony of wavering thought,
When sinners first so near are brought:
It is my Maker—dare I stay?
My SAVIOUR—dare I turn away?

Thus, while the storm is high within
'Twixt Love of CHRIST and fear of sin,
Who can express the soothing charm,
To feel Thy kind upholding Arm,

My mother Church? and hear thee tell
Of a world lost, yet loved so well,
That He, by Whom the Angels live,
His Only SON for her would give?

And doubt we yet? Thou call'st again;
A lower still, a sweeter strain;
A voice from Mercy's inmost shrine,
The very breath of Love Divine.

Whispering it says to each apart—
Come unto Me, thou trembling heart;
And we must hope, so sweet the tone,
The precious Words are all our own.

Hear them, Kind SAVIOUR, hear Thy Spouſe
Low at Thy Feet renew her vows ;
Thine own dear Promiſe ſhe would plead
For us her true though fallen ſeed.

She pleads by all her mercies, told
Thy choſen Witneſſes of old,
Love's heralds ſent to man forgiven,
One from the Croſs, and One from Heaven.

This, of true Penitents the chief,
To the loſt Spirit brings relief,
Lifting on high th' adorèd Name—
Sinners to ſave, CHRIST JESUS came.

That, deareſt of Thy boſom Friends,
Into the wavering heart deſcends—
What ? fall'n again ? yet cheerful riſe,
Thine Interceſſor never dies.

The eye of Faith that waxes bright
Each moment by Thine Altar's light
Sees them e'en now ; they ſtill abide
In Myſtery kneeling at our ſide ;

And with them every Spirit bleſt,
From realms of triumph or of reſt,
From Him Who ſaw creation's morn,
Of all Thine Angels eldeſt born,

To the poor babe, who died to-day,
Take part in our thankſgiving lay,
Watching the tearful joy and calm,
While ſinners taſte Thine Heavenly balm.

Sweet, awful hour ; the only ſound
One gentle footſtep gliding round,
Offering by turns on JESUS' part
The Croſs to every hand and heart.

Refreſh us, LORD, to hold it faſt ;
And when Thy Veil is drawn at laſt,
Let us depart where ſhadows ceaſe,
With words of Bleſſing and of Peace.

A Giving of Thanks, of the xv. Century.

Saturatus Ferculis et Cibis.

FED with Dainties from above,
　　With holieſt viands ſated,
　Nouriſhed by this Feaſt of Love,
　　With Heavenly Joys elated,
With what fitting gratitude
　Can this cold heart be glowing
To Thee, Who art here my Food,
　On me Thyſelf beſtowing ?

Now and every hour of time
　Let all Creation bleſs Thee ;
For this Feſtival ſublime
　Shall my whole heart confeſs Thee,

Who doſt thus my Spirit cheer,
    My earthly portion ſweeten,
Life revive and darkneſs clear,
    By Thy Dear Body eaten.

This through all my quickening veins
    Its ſacred Vigour poureth ;
And unto my heart and reins
    Immortal youth reſtoreth.
Oh, on what ſweet Bread to-day
    Hath my rapt Soul been feeding ;
How with thanks can I repay
    Such Love, all thanks exceeding?

Now to embrace Thy ſacred Feet
    I turn with deep affection ;
And with ſtreaming tears to greet
    The Spouſe of mine election.
Firm in faith Thy Wounds adored,
    I reckon with devotion ;
And Thy precious Death, O Lord,
    Partake with deep emotion.

Feet and Knees, Thy Hands, Thy Face,
    Heart, Eyes, Side, Boſom, viewing ;
There for Pardon and for Grace
    Bowed down and proſtrate ſuing.
May they to my heart and eyes
    For evermore be preſent ;
From my breaſt reſponſive ſighs
    To Thee draw forth inceſſant.

For thefe and Thine other Gifts
Whereof I am partaker,
Tokens of Thy Grace, I lift
My Soul to Thee, my Maker.
When in my laft earthly day,
From hence my Spirit flitteth;
And this failing frame of clay
For aye departing quitteth;

With that Sacred FLESH of Thine,
And BLOOD, my Soul deliver;
Wherein Thou, O Boon Divine,
Of Thine own Self art Giver.
May It fafe from Satan's hate,
My fhield and rampart hide me;
And to the Heavenly City's gate
In Peace and Safety guide me.

𝕿𝖍𝖊 𝕰𝖛𝖊𝖓𝖎𝖓𝖌 𝖆𝖋𝖙𝖊𝖗 𝕮𝖔𝖒𝖒𝖚𝖓𝖎𝖔𝖓.

We are members of His BODY, *of His* FLESH, *and
of His Bones.*

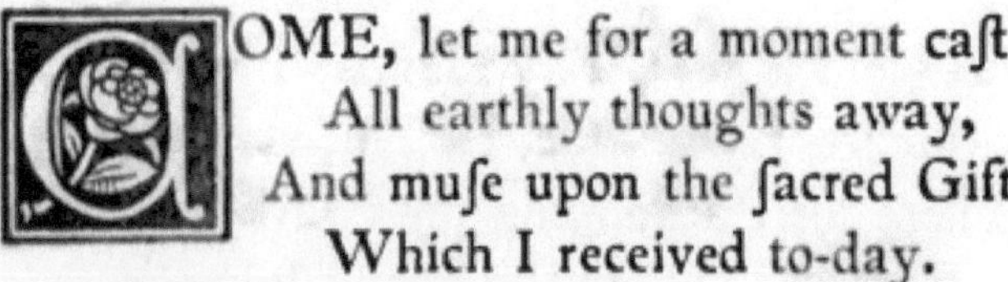

OME, let me for a moment caft
All earthly thoughts away,
And mufe upon the facred Gift
Which I received to-day.

This morning that Eternal LORD
Who is my Judge to be,
Came to this lowly tenement,
And ftayed awhile with me.

With His Celeſtial FLESH and BLOOD,
　My fainting Soul He fed ;
With tender words of Grace and Love
　My heart He comforted.

He, Who of all that live and breathe
　Is all the Life and Breath,
This morning deigned to viſit me
　In this my houſe of death.

He, Whoſe Immenſity tranſcends
　Creation's utmoſt goal,
This morning deigned to be confined
　Within my finite Soul.

He, Who in endleſs wealth abounds,
　The world's Poſſeſſor bleſt,
This morning deigned, oh, wondrous thought,
　To be by me poſſeſſed.

He, Who in Awful GODHEAD ſits
　Upon His Throne on high,
This morning entered my abode,
　In His Humanity.

He, Who for me a Trembling BABE,
　On Mary's Heart reclined,
This morning in my heart and fleſh
　His DEITY enſhrined.

O Soul of mine, reflect, reflect,
　Conſider, one by one,

What Marvels of furpaffing Grace
　　Thy God in thee has done.

His tender Love with love repay,
　　Extol His facred Name,
To all the world His Greatnefs tell,
　　His Gracioufnefs proclaim.

Euchariſtical.

Εὐχαριστοῦμέν Σοι, Δέσποτα, Κύριε, ὁ Θεὸς ἡμῶν, κ.τ.λ.

MASTER, Lord and God, to Thee
　　Thanks and adoration,
That Thou giv'ſt Thyſelf to be
　　Our Participation,
Through Thy Myſteries, Holy, Pure,
Heavenly, that for aye endure;
Souls and bodies ſtrengthening, free
　　With Thy beſt Salvation.

Loving, Bounteous, Gracious Lord,
　　Thankful we adore Thee;
May Thy Gift, on this Thy Board
　　Duly ſet before Thee,
Be to us Celeſtial Food,
Holy Body, Precious Blood—
Through Thy Spirit and Thy Word—
　　Lowly we implore Thee.

So ſhall we, with Love unblamed,
　　Godlinefs abounding,

Hope, that maketh not aſhamed,
  Faith, the Foe confounding,
Walk in Thy Commandments' way,
Till, on Thy tremendous Day,
Bleſſed we of Thee be named,
  All Thy Saints ſurrounding.

𝔈𝔲𝔠𝔥𝔞𝔯𝔦𝔰𝔱𝔦𝔠 𝔗𝔥𝔞𝔫𝔨𝔰𝔤𝔦𝔳𝔦𝔫𝔤.

O give Thanks unto the LORD, *for He is Gracious,*
  becauſe His Mercy endureth for ever.

WE give Thee thanks, Dear FATHER,
  For all Thy Glory ſhown,
In making this great Sacrifice
  For all our ſins atone ;
For giving our poor human ſight
  A SAVIOUR to adore—
Pardon and Comfort, Peace in death,
  And Life for evermore.

We thank Thee, Holy FATHER,
  For all that gentle Love,
Which leads theſe earthly, anxious hearts
  To peaceful homes above,
Which ſhows the paſſing vanity
  Of worldly cares and joys,
And man's ſtrong will and paſſions' might
  In tenderneſs deſtroys.

We give Thee thanks, Sweet SAVIOUR,
  Our grateful hearts to Thee,

Who pitieth all our ſorrows,
    And all our miſery;
We thank Thee for Thy Precious BLOOD,
    Which takes away our ſin,
Pardons our lives, our words, our deeds,
    Our inmoſt thoughts within.

O LAMB of GOD, we thank Thee
    For ſtilling all our fears,
Calming unreſtful human hearts,
    And drying all our tears;
Drawing to better, purer hopes
    Above—and Reſt in Heaven;
Whiſp'ring of never-dying Love,
    And every ſin forgiven.

We give Thee thanks, Good SPIRIT,
    For Thy Life-giving Power,
Shining with myſtic ſplendour's Light
    In Euchariſtic hour;
Oh, teach us how to worſhip GOD
    As Angels do on high,
And join our loved Communion with
    Their Altars in the Sky.

We thank Thee, HOLY SPIRIT,
    Riſe Thou within our hearts,
Illuminate the Myſtery
    This Sacrament imparts;
Oh, ſanctify the Offerings
    We bring our GOD to-day;
Reveal Thy glorious Preſence,
    And teach us how to pray.

O Triune God, we thank Thee,
  Thy glorious Name we blefs,
And afk Thy Grace to lead us on
  In paths of Holinefs ;
Help us each day to work for Thee ;
  Let not Thy Blefling ceafe ;
But ever whifper in our hearts
  The parting Words of Peace.

We give Thee thanks, O Trinity,
  Eternal Three in One,
For all the wondrous Love and Grace
  This Sacrament has won ;
We give Thee thanks, O Trinity,
  Myfterious One in Three,
For this bright Light to guide us here
  On to Eternity.

𝕽emember 𝕸e.

The Chriftian's Requeft to his Friend.

WHEN thy heart's emotion
    Yields to deep devotion,
      Oh, Friend, remember me :
    When in fweet Communion
  Loft, and facred Union,
    Oh, then remember me :
  When, from earth retiring,
  To thy Lord afpiring,
  All His Grace defiring,
    Lone thou bow'ft the knee ;

Then, when friends the deareſt
Are in Jesus neareſt,
   Then, Friend, remember me.

The Chriſtian's Requeſt to his SAVIOUR.

When, my heart beguiling,
All around is ſmiling;
   Oh, Lord, remember me :
When afflictions preſs me,
Sins and fears diſtreſs me,
   Oh, ſtill remember me :
On the couch when lying,
Languiſhing and dying;
When the laſt, laſt ſighing
   Yields my Soul to Thee ;
Then, when friends are failing,
Nought on earth availing,
   Oh, then remember me.

The SAVIOUR's Requeſt to the Chriſtian.

When, careſſed, careſſing,
Thine each earthly Bleſſing ;
   Wilt thou remember Me ?
Then, when ſunſhine fails thee,
Then, when ſtorm aſſails thee,
   Will I remember thee :
When My Word is ſpoken,
When the Bread is broken,
Of My Death the Token,
   Midſt my two or three ;

Then thy Friend, once bleeding,
Now in Glory pleading,
　　Then moſt remember Me.

When My Brethren languiſh,
Preſſed with want or anguiſh,
　　In them remember Me :
When thou hear'ſt what millions
Death's dark ſhade pavilions,
　　In them remember Me :
Think what once I ſuffered,
How My Life I offered,
How My Love diſcovered
　　Love to all, to thee :
Thus, with love's emotion,
Thus, with life's devotion,
　　Oh, thus remember Me.

Wait awhile ; be fervent ;
As My Friend and Servant
　　Awhile remember Me :
Soon ſhall faith to viſion
Yield in ſweet tranſition,
　　If thou remember Me :
Soon, with thoſe before thee
Gathered into Glory,
Thou too ſhalt adore Me,
　　Soon my Face ſhalt ſee ;
All thy faint remembrance
Loſt in bright reſemblance,
　　Oh, then remember Me.

A Poſt-Communion Prayer, of the xb. Century.

O Jesu, *Dulciſſime.*

JESU, beſt Beloved,
    Thou Bread by which we live,
Who now haſt deigned moſt really
    Thy very Self to give,
From every guilt abſolve me,
    And grant my grief to be
Sincere and penitential,
    And welcome unto Thee.

O Jesu, living Victim,
    By gifts of Grace and Love
Renew my Soul, and make me
    Acceptable above:
By broken Bread and Wine-Cup
    Eternal Life impart,
And nouriſh by Thy Preſence
    Thy Love within my heart.

Make me, Sweet Conſoler,
    All vanity to flee;
My Buckler, my Defender,
    Give me the Victory;
Teach me Thy Ways, Reſtorer,
    And grant, when Life be paſt,
In Beatific Viſion
    To ſee Thy Face at laſt.

The Remembrance.

Wie könnt ich Sein vergeſſen.

OH, how could I forget Him
    Who ne'er forgetteth me?
Or tell the Love that let Him
    Come down to ſet me free?
I lay in darkeſt ſadneſs,
    Till He made all things new,
And ſtill freſh Love and Gladneſs
    Flow from that Heart ſo true.

How could I ever leave Him,
    Who is ſo kind a Friend?
How could I ever grieve Him,
    Who thus to me doth bend?
Have I not ſeen Him dying
    For us on yonder Tree?
Do I not hear Him crying—
    Ariſe and follow Me?

For ever will I love Him,
    Who ſaw my hopeleſs plight,
Who felt my ſorrows move Him,
    And brought me Life and Light;
Whoſe Arm ſhall be around me
    When my laſt hour is come,
And ſuffer none to wound me
    Though dark the paſſage home.

He gives me Pledges holy,
   His Body and His Blood ;
He lifts the ſcorned, the lowly,
   He makes my courage good :
For He will reign within me,
   And ſhed His Graces there ;
The Heaven He died to win me
   Can I then fail to ſhare ?

In joy and ſorrow ever
   Shine through me, bleſſed Heart,
Who, bleeding for us, never
   Didſt ſhrink from ſoreſt ſmart :
Whate'er I've loved, or ſtriven,
   Or borne, I bring to Thee ;
Now let Thy Heart and Heaven
   Stand open, Lord, to me.

Act of Thankſgiving ; from the German.

Holy, Holy, Holy, Lord God *of Hoſts.*

HOLY, Holy, Thee we ſing,
   Jesu, with the Angel-throng,
Unto Thee Thy Children bring,
   Jesus, gifts of heart and ſong.
Christ, the Everlaſting God,
Christ, of Heaven the End, the Road,
Be Thou ever praiſed and bleſt,
Saviour, Lord for aye confeſt ;
Hail ! to Thee all knees are bent ;
Hail ! moſt wondrous Sacrament.

Eucharistic Adoration.

O worſhip the LORD *in the beauty of Holineſs.*

LORD, when at Thy holy Table
    We adore Thy Preſence, raiſe
Every heart, for Thou art able,
    On the wings of prayer and praiſe :
Strengthen, with the Heavenly Food
Of Thy BODY and Thy BLOOD,
All who, feeble though they be,
Come in faith to feed on Thee.

Where the Bread of Life is broken,
    Glorious is the holy place ;
Where the Word of Life is ſpoken,
    Sweet Thy reconcilèd Face :
Love and life, and faith, and prayer,
Find their deep renewal there,
All we are, or hope to be,
There we get, and give to Thee.

Myſtery of awful Wonder,
    Thou the Mighty GOD art there,
Clothed, not in Thy Robes of thunder,
    But in Love, ſo rich and rare,
That the nearer we approach,
And the more by faith we touch,
We the purer Bleſſings prove,
Higher Joy, and deeper Love.

Awful Preſence, ever filling,
    As Thou doſt, Immenſity,
Yet in all Thy Greatneſs willing
    Man's incarnate Life to be :
Oh, the fulneſs of the Bliſs
We may know through Love like this ;
Oh, the rich and precious ſtore,
Joy vouchſafed us evermore.

Hymn to the Precious Blood.

Viva, viva, Jesu.

GLORY be to Jesus,
    Who in bitter pains,
Poured for me the Life-blood
    From His ſacred Veins.

Grace and Life eternal
    In that Blood I find,
Bleſt be His Compaſſion,
    Infinitely kind.

Bleſt through endleſs ages
    Be the precious Stream,
Which from endleſs torments
    Doth the world redeem.

There the fainting Spirit
    Drinks of Life her fill ;
There, as in a fountain,
    Saves herſelf at will.

Oh, the BLOOD of CHRIST,
  It ſoothes the FATHER's Ire,
Opes the gate of Heaven,
  Quells eternal fire.

Abel's blood for vengeance
  Pleaded to the ſkies;
But the BLOOD of JESUS
  For our pardon cries.

Oft as It is ſprinkled
  On our guilty hearts,
Satan in confuſion
  Terror-ſtruck departs;

Oft as earth exulting
  Wafts its praiſe on high,
Angel Hoſts rejoicing
  Make their glad reply.

Lift ye, then, your voices;
  Swell the mighty flood;
Louder ſtill and louder,
  Praiſe the Precious BLOOD.

𝕽𝖊𝖘𝖙 𝖆𝖓𝖉 𝕻𝖊𝖆𝖈𝖊 𝖎𝖓 𝕿𝖗𝖚𝖙𝖍.

Per Pacem ad Lucem.

I DO not aſk, O LORD, that life may be
    A pleaſant road;
I do not aſk that Thou wouldſt take
    from me

Aught of its load ;
I do not ask that flowers should always spring
    Beneath my feet ;
I know too well the poison and the sting
    Of things too sweet :
For one thing only, LORD, Dear LORD, I plead,
    Lead me aright—
Though strength should falter, and though heart
        should bleed—
    Through Peace to Light.

I do not ask, O LORD, that Thou shouldst shed
    Full Radiance here ;
Give but a ray of Peace, that I may tread
    Without a fear ;
I do not ask my Cross to understand,
    My way to see—
Better in darkness just to feel Thy Hand
    And follow Thee.
Joy is like restless day ; but Peace Divine,
    Like quiet night :
Lead me, O LORD—till perfect Day shall shine,
    Through Peace to Light.

A Sacramental Retrospect.

Worthy is the LAMB *That was slain.*

OH, moments of feeling, how sacred, how
    sweet,
    When, with JESUS amidst them, His
    " two or three" meet ;

His Love's farewell Tokens to each one are given:
O Holy Communion, O foretaſte of Heaven.

Hark, hark to thoſe accents—In Mem'ry of Me,
Eat, drink; 'tis My Body, My Blood; 'tis for
      thee—
Each heart, like that Body, is broken for ſin;
Like that Blood, in devotion 'tis poured out
      within.

All that's earthly has vaniſhed, ſin, ſorrow, and
      fear;
'Tis Jesus abſorbs us, He only is here:
What Peace, paſt expreſſion, His Peace, fills the
      mind;
While to love each emotion, His Love, is reſigned.

O'er each boſom His Spirit deſcends, like a Dove;
All pride, all unkindneſs, is melted in Love:
So ſweetly affianced, as ſinners undone,
To Thee, Dying Saviour, Thy Love makes us
      one.

Yet we mourn that, too often, in breaking Thy
      Bread,
Thou art known, as Thou once wert, and ſuddenly
      fled:
Our hearts, in Thy Preſence, oh, did they not burn?
But too brief was that fervour, too ſlow to return.

Yet, lovely Memorials, what ſtill ye record,
In thoſe hearts is engraven the Death of our Lord:
Till, with all His redeemed ones, we ſwell the
       glad ſtrain—
How worthy, all worthy, the Lamb that was ſlain.

The Sign of the Son of Man.

*Then ſhall appear the Sign of the Son of Man
in Heaven.*

CROSS, O Croſs of Shame,
   In every age the ſame,
   Thou Symbol of a ſhameful thing,
   Meet for a ſlave, and not a King;
Symbol of ſhame and loſs,
Where is thy Grace, O Croſs,
That I ſhould bear thee thus with heart and hand,
Where earth's rude ſcorners ſtand—
Myſelf a laughing-ſtock for thee,
A by-word, and a mockery?

O Croſs, O Croſs of Pain,
Where is to me the gain,
That in this bleeding heart of mine,
I nail each bitter nail of thine,
That ſtill with every breath
I live a life of death—
A life, that is a daily dying ſtill,
A death, that may not kill;

But hour by hour, and day by day,
Feeds on the life it will not ſlay?

O Croſs, O Croſs of Light,
With Heavenly beauty bright,
I love and glory in thy ſhame,
For He, I love, has borne the ſame.
The world may ſcorn and threat
Her idle vengeance yet;
But I will bear thee ſtill with heart and hand,
Though men with devils band;
For He, I love, is with me ſtill,
And ſhame is ſweet, if His dear Will.

O Croſs, O Croſs of Joy,
Oh, Sweetneſs without cloy,
Still wound and pierce my bleeding heart,
For honey ſtreams from every dart.
O crimſon, crimſon Tree,
Still let me cling to thee;
For thy dear arms repoſing day by day,
Still let me die alway;
For He, I love, is by my ſide,
And death is ſweet, for He has died.

O Croſs, O Croſs of Woe,
When Heaven and earth ſhall glow,
When blazing in the eaſtern ſky,
The Son of Man's dread Sign ſhall lie,
His Sign, no more of ſhame,
His Croſs, a Croſs of flame,

To whom the gain, to whom the endleſs loſs,
    At that dread Day, O Croſs,
To ſcorner, or to ſcorned, on high?
    The Fire ſhall try . . . . the Fire ſhall try.

Jeſus paſſeth by.

Jesus *of Nazareth paſſeth by.*

THOU paſſeſt by—Thy awful Step I hear;
    Thou paſſeſt by—Thy five dread
       Wounds I ſee;
    Thou paſſeſt by—Thy ſaving Croſs I
       claſp
With penitential tears of agony.

Thou paſſeſt by—I will not let Thee go
    Until Thy Mercy ſtreams into my Soul;
I am ſin-laden; lift the burden off,
    For Thou alone canſt heal and make me whole.

Renew my Spirit with unſwerving faith,
    While pondering on the path Thy Saints have
       trod;
With hope and courage nerve this feeble frame
    To follow Thee, Thou Ever-preſent GOD.

Thou paſſeſt by—I pray to be illumed
    With Grace and Light; ſo ſhall the darkneſs
       flee:
And theſe dim eyes, O Thou Aſcended LORD,
    In rapture recogniſe and gaze on Thee.

The Second Advent.

Ye do show the Lord's *Death till He come.*

BY Christ redeemed, in Christ reſtored,
We keep the Memory adored,
And ſhow the Death of our **Dear Lord,**
Until **He come.**

His Body broken in our ſtead,
Is here, in this Memorial Bread—
And ſo our feeble love is fed,
Until He come.

His fearful Drops of Agony,
His Life-blood ſhed for us we ſee—
The Wine ſhall tell the Myſtery,
Until He come.

And thus **that dark** betrayal-night,
With **the laſt** Advent we unite—
The ſhame, the Glory, by this **Rite,**
Until **He come.**

Until the Trump of God be heard,
Until the ancient graves be ſtirred,
And with the great commanding Word,
The Lord ſhall come.

O bleſſed Hope, with this elate
Let not our hearts be deſolate,
But ſtrong in faith, in patience wait,
Until He come.

A Hymn on the Heavenward Courſe; of the xviii. Century.

Himmelan geht unſre Bahn.

HEAVENWARD ſtill our pathway tends,
　　Here on earth we are but ſtrangers,
Till our road in Canaan ends,
　　Through this wilderneſs of dangers;
Here we but as pilgrims rove,
For our Home is there above.

Heavenward ſtill my Soul aſcend,
　　Thou art one of Heaven's creations;
Earth can ne'er give aim or end
　　Fit to fill thy aſpirations;
　　And a Heaven-enlightened mind
　　Ever turns its ſource to find.

Heavenward ſtill, GOD calls to me,
　　In His Word ſo clearly ſpeaking;
Glimpſes in that Word I ſee
　　Of the Home I'm ever ſeeking;
　　And while that my ſteps defends,
　　Still to Heaven my track aſcends.

Heavenward ſtill my thoughts ariſe,
  When He to His Board invites me ;
Then my Spirit upward flies,
  Foretaſte then of Heaven delights me :
    When on earth this Food has ceaſed,
    Comes the LAMB's Own Marriage-feaſt.

Heavenward ſtill my Spirit wends,
  That fair land by faith exploring ;
Heavenward ſtill my heart aſcends,
  Sun, and moon, and ſtars out-ſoaring :
    Their faint rays in vain would try
    With the light of Heaven to vie.

Heavenward ſtill when life ſhall cloſe,
  Death to my true Home ſhall guide me ;
There, triumphant o'er my woes,
  Laſting Bliſs ſhall GOD provide me :
    CHRIST Himſelf the way has led,
    Joyful in His Steps I tread.

Still then Heavenward, Heavenward ſtill,
  That ſhall be my watchword ever ;
Heaven's delights my heart ſhall fill,
  And from vain illuſions ſever :
    Heavenward ſtill my thoughts ſhall run,
    Till the gate of Heaven I've won.

Prayer for the Gift of Gratitude.

Aus Lieb verwundter, Jesu *mein.*

JESU, Pierced for love of me,
How can this poor heart grateful be?
Would that my burning love might be
Even as is Thy Love to me.
Now on a wondrous wife doft Thou
Thy very Self on me beftow:
Love bids Thee ftoop to be fo low—
But who that depth of Love can know?

Oh, come to me, Dear LORD, I pray,
And let Thy Love my Spirit ftay:
Behold, it longeth fore for Thee,
I would it might more worthy be.
To foreft ftreams the Hart doth hie,
When he for thirft is fain to die;
And fo my Soul doth pant for Thee,
O JESU, JESU, come to me.

I cannot love Thee as I would,
Yet pardon me, O Higheft Good;
My life, and all I call mine own,
I lay before Thine Altar-Throne:
And if a thoufand lives were mine,
O Sweeteft LORD, they fhould be Thine;
And fcanty would the offering be,
So richly haft Thou loved me.

Act of Reparation; a Sequence of the xvii. Century.

Plange, Sion, muta vocem.

SION, mourn, thy voice ſubduing,
　　Turn to lamentation, viewing
　　　　All men's wild and fearful rage:
　　Loving greatly, greatly wailing,
Praiſe thy God, though ſin prevailing
　　　　Lively hate in thee engage.

Joy in God now well thou leaveſt,
Nor that ſacred Food receiveſt
　　Which makes life to live indeed:
He with ſtripes again is goaded,
And with deep reproaches loaded,
　　Who to ſave us came to bleed.

Oh, how vile was the commiſſion,
How abhorred the repetition
　　Of the Croſs, that deed of ſhame:
His betray, deny Him, and flee apace;
Captain, King, Prieſt, ſoldier, and populace
　　For the death of God exclaim.

What the Love of God has lent us,
And for our Salvation ſent us,
　　Into judgment here is turned:
Here the Holy is profanèd;
Here the Word of Truth diſdainèd;
　　With contempt the Good is ſpurned.

He, the LAMB, Heaven's Adoration,
In the Altar's pure Oblation,
　　Can but low efteem fecure:
Light to Heaven, here darkly hidden;
Praifed above, here rudely bidden
　　Contradiction to endure.

Who in Heaven with jubilation,
Here, in bitter indignation
　　Stand, the Meffengers of light.
Howl, ye foes of GOD, and tremble,
Nor your dread of Him diffemble,
　　Sinners, when He comes in Might.

Sheep and goats, of diverfe fpirits,
Find Him tempered to their merits;
　　Due rewards to each He deals:
CHRIST, Himfelf our Victim giving,
Is the Judge of all men living;
　　And e'en now their fentence feals.

Doth this fpeech your dread awaken,
Thundered forth by faith unfhaken?
　　Hear a fpeech more ftern and dread—
With Me ye fhall enter never,
Nor My Banquet tafte for ever—
　　Thus the unchanging King hath faid.

Still He looks 'mid guefts reclining,
'Mid fo many veftures fhining,
　　If there be one naked found:

Oh, what weight of chains ſhall bind him,
What a miſt of darkneſs blind him,
  Given up to torments, bound.

Many ſhall in Hell awaken,
By the ſleep of death o'ertaken,
  Guilty of the FLESH of CHRIST.
Whither are ye blindly going?
Now the Vine is Life beſtowing,
  Why are ye to death enticed?

LORD, to whom ſhall we retiring
Go from Thee, his face deſiring,
There with better hopes enquiring—
  Thou the Truth, the Life, the Way?
Lo! we ſtand, in terror ſuing,
And our ſtubborn Souls ſubduing,
Praiſe and ſorrow both renewing,
  Proſtrate hearts before Thee lay.

On us Thy Rebuke is turnèd,
When Thou with contempt art ſpurnèd;
And our hearts with anger burnèd
  When Thy foes were thus profane.
Gentle LAMB, Propitiation
For the ſinful world's Salvation:
Mourned we Thine Humiliation;
  Thou their wickedneſs reſtrained.

Stop the mouth that Thee blaſphemeth,
Heal the mind that falſely deemeth,

Stay the hand that vile esteemeth,
Trust not love that only seemeth,
    Make Thy Fear on all to seize.
While we view this profanation,
What can check our lamentation?
Lo! ourselves are Thy Oblation;
Sighs and tears our aspiration,
    Grant us, which Thyself may please.

The Completion of the Sacrifice of the Cross.

It is finished.

IT is finished—Jesus said,
Bowing on the Cross His Head.
It is finished—He says now
When the voice comes soft and low:
Lo! the Victim's FLESH and BLOOD—
Eat and drink with gratitude.

But if any would have part,
They must sorrow with That Heart;
Then, if Jesus thus be given,
They must render back to Heaven
Holy thanks of heart and will,
Else it is unfinished still.

Were it from my heart alone
Praise ascended to Thy Throne,

Were there not within its fhrine
More than earthly Bread and Wine,
Then, O then, it could not blefs
Save by owning thankleffnefs.

But there entered this fweet hour
To my heart heart-changing Power ;
Now that inner Aid I claim,
All within me, praife GOD's Name ;
Thou didft teach Thine Own to pray,
Teach me now to praife and fay—

Wake, my glory ; wake, fweet ftring ;
I myfelf will wake and fing ;
Lo! my heart forgets its care,
For my Love hath entered there,
And its only thought is this—
He is mine, and I am His.

What the Fathers longed to fee,
And the Prophets' company,
What the holy Kings long dead
Their true Crown had reckonèd,
The moft holy Bread of Heaven—
This to me is freely given.

What the people on the fhore
Prayed might feed them evermore,
What the woman by the well
Afked, that fhe might thirftlefs dwell,

S

This is rendered to our need—
Meat indeed and Drink indeed.

Who ſhall meaſure out Its price ?
Who for It make ſacrifice ?
Gold or rubies gauge It never,
All from all for It may ſever,
And though nought to yield remain
Infinite would be their gain.

Therefore with all Hoſts on high—
Alleluia !—rapt I cry ;
Praiſe to Him, Who from the Higheſt
Hath to lowly Souls come nigheſt ;
Sing of Him till time is o'er,
Alleluia ! evermore.

𝕴𝖓𝖉𝖊𝖝

OF THE SOURCES OF THE HYMNS.

PART I.

No. 1.

ORIGINAL Tranflation by A. M. M. Daniel's Thefaurus Hymnologicus. 1855-6. Date uncertain.

2. Hymns. By F. W. Faber, D.D. Richardfon. New Ed. 1862. From the Italian.

3. Hymns from the Land of Luther. Kennedy. New Ed. 1862. Tranflated from the German of E. Liedich by H. L. L. xviij Century.

4. The Old Church Porch. Edited by Rev. W. J. E. Bennett, M.A. Anonymous.

5. Lauda Syon : Ancient Latin Hymns of the Englifh and other Churches ; Tranflated into correfponding Metres, by J. D. Chambers, M.A. Recorder of New Sarum. Mafters. 1857. From a Munich MS. Mone's Hymni Latini Medii Ævi. 1853.

6. Hymns of the Heart. By Matthew Bridges, Efq. Richardfon. 2nd Ed. 1851.

7. Out and Home : Memorials of the late Rev. W. G. Tupper, M.A. Edited by his Brother. Bofworth and Harrifon. 2nd Ed. 1856.

---

* In the firft reference to a Work, the title is given at full length : afterwards, it is abridged.

8. Original Tranſlation by W. A.   The Divine Liturgy.
   Edited by Rev. Orby Shipley, M. A.   Maſters.
   2nd Thouſand.   1863.   From the York Proceſ-
   ſional.   Daniel's Theſaurus.   Date uncertain.

9. Original Tranſlation by Frances Elizabeth Cox.   From
   the German of Rambach.   xviij Century.

10. Original Tranſlation by A. M. M.   The Divine Li-
    turgy.   From the Drontheim Miſſal.   Sequentiæ ex
    Miſſalibus.   Edited by J. M. Neale, M. A.   J. W.
    Parker.   1852.

11. Original Hymn by J. H.   The Divine Liturgy.

12. Poems.   By Dean Alford.   Rivington.   New Ed. 1859.

13. Chambers' Lauda Syon.   From a Munich MS.

14. Original Poem by C. S.

15. After Cowper, by H. R. B.

16. Maſque of Mary, and other Poems: by E. Caſwall.
    Burns and Lambert.   1858.

17. Original Tranſlation by A. M. M.   Daniel's Theſau-
    rus.   Date uncertain.

18. Original Hymn by W. E.

19. Lyra Germanica: Second Series; The Chriſtian Life.
    Tranſlated from the German by Catherine Wink-
    worth.   Longman.   4th Ed. 1861.   A Hymn of
    Angelus (J. Scheffler).   xvij Century.

20. Original Hymn by B.

21. May Carols.   By Aubrey de Vere, Eſq.   Longman.
    1857.

22. Hymns from the Land of Luther.   From the German
    of Count Zinzendorf.   xviij Century.

23. Euchariſtic Hymns: now firſt tranſlated.   Edited by
    a Committee of Clergy.   Palmer.   1862.   From
    a MS. at Mayence.   By L.

24. A Chaplet of Verſes.   By Adelaide A. Proĉter.   Long-
    man.   1862.

25. The Paſſion of JESUS.   By M. Bridges, Eſq.   Rich-
    ardſon.   1852.

26. Lyra Germanica.   From the German of J. Heermann.
    xvij Century.

27. Hymns of the Eaſtern Church.   By J. M. Neale,
    D. D.   Hayes.   2nd Ed. 1863.

28. The Omnipreſence of GOD, and other Sacred Poems.
    By Rev. T. Grinfield.   1824.

PART V.

Index

OF THE FIRST LINES OF THE HYMNS.